The Dust Bubble

D NASIR

Order this book online at www.trafford.com/07-1909
or email orders@trafford.com

Most Trafford titles are also available at major online book retailers.

Edited by: Aisha Morris
Cover Artwork by: David Shafeek

Note for Librarians: A cataloguing record for this book is available from Library and Archives Canada at www.collectionscanada.ca/amicus/index-e.html

ISBN: 978-1-4251-4511-8

www.trafford.com

North America & international
toll-free: 1 888 232 4444 (USA & Canada)
phone: 250 383 6864 • fax: 250 383 6804
email: info@trafford.com

The United Kingdom & Europe
phone: +44 (0)1865 722 113 • local rate: 0845 230 9601
facsimile: +44 (0)1865 722 868 • email: info.uk@trafford.com

10 9 8 7 6 5 4 3 2

Acknowledgements

All Praise to my Creator, The One True God

Thanks to Starr Lane Ventures Productions, Inc. for believing in me and my talent enough to sponsor my book

Special thanks to my mother,
Willa Pearl

*This book is dedicated to my daughter,
Daneika, and to Aisha*

Prologue

The Dust Bubble is a brilliant novel, full of family, immediate and extended, love, hope and nostalgia. It's about a community pulling together with a common goal; guiding a fatherless boy through childhood into manhood.

The term, Dust Bubble, comes from an old saying: My mouth is so dry I could blow a dust bubble. But 'The Dust Bubble' here has nothing to do with the dryness of mouth.

The story is set in the 70's when neighborhoods were more than the areas you lived in, they were the precincts of extended family. There was an axiom in place then, taken from an African proverb, which said, It takes a village to raise a child. When, everyone in the hood helped raise every child. It was a time when People helped people.

The Dust Bubble

Chapter 1

The Heart Attacks

My daddy died when I was 8 years old. Him and my momma were truly in love. What I know about love I learned from watching the two of them together. When they held hands I really believe that they became one solitary person. Momma laughed a lot when daddy was near. Daddy glowed when he was with us. When he died Momma stopped laughing. The insurance was current and because Daddy's death was accidental the insurance company paid Momma double indemnity. She dressed Daddy in a steel grey tailor-made suit that he had just been fitted for. I know that it should have been in the lay-away for at least 6 months. Daddy said it was too expensive but Momma made him have it cut. She said that he never did anything for himself.

The funeral was held on the 7th day after Daddy died. It was a large service, a lot of people liked Daddy, he was a real good man. At the time, I didn't understand how come everybody cried so hard, especially Momma. When she got the call from the police she came into my room, sat on the bed and called me to her side.

"Boo Boo," she said, "come sit by Momma."

"Look at my plane."

"Not now Sweetheart, listen, you know Momma told you that Heaven was the best place in the whole world?"

"Yep, an' God has a throne there with Angels an' clouds."

"That's right Boo, an' remember when I told you that everybody has their own time when they go to God?"

"Like when big Gran' Ma went?"

"That's right honey. Well they just called an' said that your Daddy has gone to Heaven like Big Grand Mother."

"But I thought he went to work."

"He did Boo Boo, but on his way home he was in an accident an' him an' three other people died. They all went to Heaven with Daddy."

"Are we goin' to put him in the ground next to big Gran' Ma?"

"Yes, we are."

At nights, in bed, I'd wake up cause I'd hear Momma crying, calling Daddy's name. The first time I heard her I ran into her room but he wasn't there, she was talking to his picture. I didn't know what to do so I just went back to my room and listened to her cry. At the graveyard she was worse than she was all those nights. She fell down on the pile of dirt and cried out,

"Oh Lord! God! Dear God, why now? Not now Lord!" That's what I couldn't understand then. Momma told me that Heaven was the best place in the whole world and God watches over all of His flock so I thought that Momma should have been smiling and singing. I realized then that kids weren't supposed to understand grown stuff. I don't know, but I guess that my time will be close at hand when I do.

I watched the gentlemen and the preacher raise Momma up from the dirt. I saw all of the people looking at me. Miss Elisha took me in her arms and held me close to her while everybody tried to calm Momma down. Her tears deluged down her face like the rain that fell at big Gran' Ma's funeral.

That was a long time ago, now I'm just past 13. The big part of Momma's insurance money is gone; she had to take a secretary job so she could support us. She didn't mind doing it at all. She told me that I was her world and she'd do what she had to do to make things okay for us. I told her I was going to get a job one day and take care of her. She kissed me right on the mouth, just like she does when she's real happy, an' told me that she knew I'd keep my promise.

I tried to get a job at McDonald's, they're the first ones to tell me that I needed to be 16 even to get a work permit. I didn't want to wait for three years so I tried other places, other things. I cut grass, raked leaves, washed cars for $2.50 each. I saved all of the money that I made. Then my Momma said she couldn't take the money even though I made it to help her. She told me to save it so I could have a head start on life.

I did some of everything I could do to make money because my Daddy used to say that the men should take care of the women folk, that's how he met my Momma. He said that some guy hit Momma and he beat the guy up then took Momma to dinner. It sounded real pretty when he told it. They'd been together ever since that time. Momma said she loved his sense of humor, said that he was real gentle but every bit a man. I want to be that type of man when I grow up. I guess that I better start working on my sense of humor now!

Archibald is my friend's name, he's got a big family and a sense of humor so I like hanging with him. He's got one sister, Carmel, who is a stone brick house. She's about 25 and I know that I'm dead wrong checking her out but, man! She's what we call Hot Property. She'll put on a mini skirt, halter top and go-go boots and it'll drive me crazy-crazy! I think she knows it cause when I'm there she always comes in and sits on Archie's lap. She'll give me these looks where she licks her lips, then she'll adjust her halter, I don't know, I guess that the boobs be making it slide down or something but it always makes my eyes pop open and I get a tingling feeling down there.

Me and Arch always leave his house laughing and talking stuff after she does her tease-thang. He told me she started sitting on his lap and patting his butt after he walked in on her and her ex, buck-necked getting wild! He walked in and froze in his tracks.

While he was standing there with his mouth wide open she just said, “Gone in the kitchen an’ get yourself somethin’ to eat Sweetheart. Arch, close the door Honey.” He said that she was so beautiful that he forgot that she was his sister. Said he hadn’t ever seen a grown woman naked, I still haven’t, shoot, he’s lucky. Me and him trip off of Carmel then we hit the streets and peep out the chicks. Sometimes we’d be so messed up behind Carmel that we’d walk all the way across town to be with these two girls. Their names were Sugar Roo and Sugar Ree, I don’t know where Arch met them but they were not nasty, they were nicety. Their mother was always gone so they didn’t have a problem taking us to her big old bed where we would get our feel game on. They knew how to kiss and roll. We never did take off our clothes or anything but it felt so good we didn’t care. That was the closest thing to sex to us.

One day we stayed over too long, it was 11:00 when we looked up. We knew that we were going to be killed so we took some alley-way-short-cuts home. It was some of that cutting through alleys, jumping over fences, running through people’s yards going on when we met Pretty Penni, September, and Ana Stasia. We didn’t know their names but we knew they were thoroughbred. No lie! They were going into the back door of a building that used to be a warehouse. The windows were boarded up and there was a red light above the door.

We hurried up to where they were so we could get a close look at them. They were all dressed the same, wearing gold bellbottoms, black halters and black platforms. Pretty Penni had a huge Angela Davis Afro, Ana Stasia had Afro puffs, and September had either a perm or a straight wig. They were all so tight that me and Arch just walked up to them and stared. Ana Stasia asked us,

“What you little cutie pies doin’ out here so late?” We were froze, locked in a crystal of time. Then September spoke up,

“Hey Baby Boy, you hear Ana talkin’ to you?”

“Oh, yeah, we on our way home.”

“Y’all better be. Somebody might snatch ya’ll little asses up an’ make a light snack outta y’all”.

Pretty Penni jumped in, her voice was so soft and smooth,

"Hey cut them some slack girls, look at 'em standin' there with they mouths all open an' they little thangs throbbin' in them polyesters".

They all laughed, we both reached down to cover our stuff.

"Look at 'em! What's y'alls names?

"People call me Bones."

"On Bone? Ha, ha, ha!"

"What about you Peachie?"

"My name is Archibald."

"Your thang art bald? Ha, ha, ha!"

"Naw, little cats, we just funnin'! We're a singin' group, we're called the Heart Attacks. You know what this place is don't you?"

"No"

"This is the Dust Bubble, I'm September, that's Ana Stasia, an' that hootchie is Pretty Penni."

"We heard of the Heart Attacks!"

"Maybe one day you'll be lucky enough to hear us sing. How old are y'all?" "We're 13….we're 14" busted out at the same time.

"Naw! He said 13! I heard him!"

"We 13."

"You wanna be 14, huh Archibald?"

"Naw, I just wanna be your 13 year old man. Can I have a chance?"

Everybody laughed.

"Boy, you are so cute! Hey y'all, it's gettin' late, we gotta get in. Hey, we gone be on the bandstand at Circle T Park on the 15th. Y'all come, and' tell a lot of y'all friends an' we'll dedicate a song to y'all, cool?"

"That's a groove!"

"Yeah, that's fly!"

"Okay, y'all get ta' steppin'! Let's sing 'em off girls."

They snapped their fingers three times and sung,

"Bye Bye Baby, it's time to go, Don't mean maybe, end of the show,

Ba da da Ba da da Boom! *See ya!"* They all broke out laughing.

"Bye Ana Stasia. Bye Pretty Penni!"

"Bye September!"

They hit the buzzer, the door opened, they blew more kisses and went in giggling. We gave each other 5 on the black hand side and took off towards home. We were tripping all the way to the crib. We had just met the finest Bricks on the planet? We knew that on the 15th that we were going to be off the hook! That was if we didn't die that night from butt whoopings. We came down Euclid to Marsh to the corner where we'd split up and go home. Our grins faded when we got to the top of the key, we knew it was late and we knew that we were dead wrong. Then we went back to the grinning because the thought of Sugar Roo and Sugar Ree then the Heart Attacks was enough to over ride any thought of butt whooping!

At the corner the 'tude keep switching. Till it felt like somebody kicked the bucket. At last we dropped our heads, drooped our shoulders, and got ready for the drama.

"Man, I'll see you at school tomorrow, that's probably the only time we'll get to see each other. But I can't wait to tell all them jive turkeys about tonight!"

"I mean! But e'rybody gone be trippin' on us till the 15th!"

"Aw, snap! What if we both get 2 weeks punishment for tonight, we'll miss the show!"

"Dang!"

"It's a hurtin' thang!"

"Yeah. I'll catch you later." 5 down low.

"Be cool Cat."

"Be cool." 5 on the white hand side.

The timer on our living room lamp had the front of the house lit up but Momma's bedroom light wasn't on. I knew she wouldn't have went to bed while I was out so I started feeling better. I went in and found a note from her saying that she had to work a double which meant that she would be out until about 1 or 1:30. I lucked up! Her note told me to fix myself something to eat and to forgive her for not being there. Man! That was a groove! I ate me a cheese and mushroom omelet and had a slice of Momma's Chocolate Angel pie. I put on the Isley Brothers, "*3 plus 3*", and grooved to the "*Who's That Lady*" side. As I listened to the sounds I just sat and thought about the ladies, all of them!

The next day me and Archie met outside on the schoolyard before the bell rang, it was going to be one of those pretty days, I could just tell. Kevin, Ricky, Duh-Duh, Sheila, and Theresa, shoot, everybody was out there. We started telling Ricky and Duh-Duh about Sugar Roo and Sugar Ree when everybody started pulling up on us. Duh-Duh broke in,

"Tttttell 'em 'bout ttttthem ssssssugar gals!"

"Aw man! Check it out, them slim goodies is fine! First Arch is groovin' off of Sugar Roo then I got Sugar Ree, man, we grindin' an' swappin' spit an' I got my hands workin' like Octapussy bro!"

"But check it out Rick, we on the way to the pad bustin' through the alleys an' Boom! We run into them sexy ass Heart Attacks."

"Hell naw! Get otta here with that shit!"

"Ricky man, if I'm lyin' I'm flyin'! Check, check, check September...."

"September, who the fuck is that?"

"Chill out man, you all cussin' an' thangs. September is one of the Hearts, she fine man."

"Shoot, they all fine!"

"An' y'all know 'em?"

"They tell us they gone do a show at the Circle on the 15th, they say tell our friends an' they gone dedicate a song to us. Us man!"

"Man you trippin'!"

"Hey Kevin man, it's all good! Dreams ain't never changed into nothin' real. We gone be at the park on the 15th. What's happenin'?"

"Awright, cause I'm feeling' you I'm with y'all! What time we steppin'?"

"I heard on 104 W.H.E.P. that the ban' go on at 4, let's meet up in front of the church at 2 so we can get there before the first set, cool?"

"Shoot! Let's walk that walk!"

"Me an' Yogi goin' with y'all. Y'all ain't leavin' the girls out this time!"

"I hear ya. I'm wearin' my Levis an' Chuck Taylors. I'm gone be right down front when Ana Stasia call my name baby boy!"

The bell rang and we went into homeroom. Everybody was tripping about the thing at the park all day. They had been hearing about it on the radio and now that me and Archie's name was tied up in it, we were like stars in school. Chicks were coming up to me screaming about catching me at the park and talking about how they heard through the grapevine that I was grinding on September's sister Sugar Ree. I mean! They can get some stories tied up. They turned me into a star and I wasn't even going to be on stage.

Still I wasn't mad. During the 4th period gym class, Mr. Gates, the teacher, came to me giving me five, talking about he heard that I knew the Heart Attacks. He said that he saw them once at Fat Man's, said he didn't know how I knew them but it was too bad that I was so young because they were hot! I told him to come to the park and I would introduce him to all three of them. Then I started thinking,

"I don't e'en know if they still remember me."

Shoot, I hoped so, them foxes had me loco. I just wanted to see them one more time. I thought I was going to be signing autographs before the day was over but I didn't. What I did do was get three phone numbers, one was from Kendall. I had been trying to get under her skin since September the 10th.

Saturday, May 15th, finally came and you should have seen me, I was up all Friday night pressing and creasing my Levis. It was going to be hot at the park in more than a hundred ways. When it was 20 minutes till two I was just finishing up 4 pieces of chicken, mashed potatoes and gravy, hot cornbread and I drank a Pepsi. When I got to the church next to 'Arch's house there were about 14 or 15 people there.

"Man, We was gone leave yo' ass."

"What? I live less than a block from here an' nobody could come an' get me? That's foul!"

"Chill out dude, you know you that thang! Shoot, you an' Arch hooked!"

"Y'all hang on while I go up in there an' get him outta the crib. He probably in there stuffin' his mug."

"Hurry up man, we ready to roll!"

"Well go ahead."

"Pshh! We'll be here!"

I knocked on the door hoping that Carmel would open it. I was floating on nine. The Heart Attacks had me thinking I was the stuff. Like I was some kind of Mack. The chicks and even the cats in the neighborhood started treating me like I was Max Jullian. That's heavy. Ricky and Kevin were on the B. ball team and all of the chicks dug them but now Ricky's ex, Theresa, is digging me.

"What's up cat?"

"Hey Bones, come on in. I'm just finishing up this burger an' fries, you want some?"

"Naw, I'm cool! Hurry up so we can split. I'm in a hurry to see Pretty Penni!"

"Pretty? Man. You know that's me!"

"Awright, that leaves Ana Stasia an' September for me, dude!"

"September is hot!"

"I'm sayin'! An' Ana Stasia got that ass! Did you peep that?"

"That an' them lips. Man, I bet she can kiss her ass off!"

"I'm sayin' I'd give my left nut to touch that ass though!"

"Ha ah ha! She got some sexy lips, when they sung that song to us, I dreamed about them that night an' woke up on bone!"

"Man, I did too!"

"Shut up! That was a piss hard on!"

"Goofy! Let's go. I wonder if Kevin an' nim showed up yet."

"Buggin'? There's 15 people out there waitin' for us."

"What? Why didn't you say so?"

"Man, they probably been out there since 12."

"You see Yogi?"

"Kevin's girl?"

"Yep."

"Yeah, she out there, why?"

"Pshh!"

"Hecky naw!"

"For real!"

"Gone with ya bad self! Let's raise!"

We tripped all the way to the park. Everybody was asking us to tell the story over and over and over, then we had to sing the "Good-night" song umpteen times. We went in A& P where Kevin, Pig, and Peabody did some five finger discounting. They got a 5th of Thunderbird and some grape Kool-ade. The Kool-ade turned the Bird into pure grape wine. Since Kevin lifted the bottle he took the "poison" off. That was the longest swig of anybody that day, he passed the bottle to Peabody then to Pig, it ended up going around three times to every one of us. When Lucy took her first swig she coughed and the Bird flew out of her nose. We all cracked up. The bottle was enough to get everybody blitzed but we still went past Yogi's big brother's weed house. He gave us a slim stick of Acapulco Gold that had us tripping.

By the time we stumbled up on the Circle it was jam-packed. We had to fight our way through the park. We got lucky though we got a bench in the second row, it wasn't anybody sitting there except a big lady with a wig and some Daisy Dukes on. I think it was a lady. Anyway, Pig nodded out before the girls even came out to do their show. He knew that we would wake him up before the thump got underway.

We were just tripping when September walked past the stage. Man, me an' Arch was gone. He snatched me up and made me run to her.

"September! September!"

"Hey! Look who's here! On Bone an' Bald Thang! Just kiddin'! Come here!"

She kissed both of us on the cheeks and our whole row was dying!

She asked us to come to the dressing room with her. Arch's face lit up.

"Hey girls, look who I found!"

"The young tenders! Where's my hug Bones?"

"Hi, Ana Stasia!"

I hugged her and she slapped me on the butt! Aw man, there is a God in Heaven who answers prayers!

"Hey! Is she the only one you see?"

"Hi, Pretty Penni!" I hugger her too.

"So you dudes got dates?"

"We brought about 15 people with us. We in the second row with some big lady with a wig an' some pink hot pants."

"Ha, ha, ah! That ain't no girl. That's Miss Tur's ex, Dirty Diana."

"Who's mister?"

"No, Miss ---- Tur, that's the bartender at the Bubble. So do you two want a job?"

"Job? Yeah!" We busted out at the same time.

"Okay, I'm gone take y'all out to the car an' I want y'all to bring all of the cases and bags, cool?"

"Okay, let's go."

"Sept, have 'em get the make up bag on the first trip Honey."

"Penni, did you bring your flask?"

"Yeah, it's in the blue make up case."

We made three rips to the car, when we got back from the last trip they were dressed in silver elephant leg bellbottoms. They had on blue patent-leather stacks and red satin blouses with the bellbottom sleeves and ruffles down front. They looked like something out of dreams. Ana Stasia came up with the idea to have us escort them on stage once they were announced. I was going nutty inside. Me and Arch jumped up and started camel-walking, slapped 5 on the black hand side then 5 real slow.

Pretty Penni stopped us because there was only about 5 minutes before they had to hit the stage. I was to have Pretty on my left, Ana

Stasia on my right and Arch would bring September out.

When we heard the comedian getting his last laughs somebody knocked on the door and said, "one minute." I was ready for Pretty! Sept opened the door and we heard the announcement by Stan, The Ladies Man.

"Ladies an' germs, you've all been so kind especially when you laughed at my Viet Nam Joke!" Laughter ensued. "Now, I've been all across the country but I ain't never saw a group of women as lovely as these three. Ladies an' Gentlemen, show 'em you dig 'em! The Beautiful an' talented, Heart Attacks!!!!"

My heart started racing like 90 in the 55 mile an hour zone. Pretty said she could feel my heart and knew the feeling. She told me to calm down and just get it on. Arch and Sept walked down to the other end and paused. Sept gave us a nod and we all hit the stage together. They came on stage right and we came on from the left. We walked the ladies on and exited from opposite directions we came on. The crowd was ballistic, no lie, it felt like they were applauding us but they were really cheering for the Hearts.

(Except our row of friends and Dirty Diana.) Sept took the mike and said, "Ladies and Gentlemen please give it up for our escorts, Arch an' Bones. This first song is dedicated to them, it's called "Sukiaki"

"*It's all because of you, I'm feelin' sad an' blue, you went away..........*"

She sung Taste of Honey's song like she was born to do that. Me and Arch dug the scene from stage left. We got weak when Pretty hit her highs. Tears came right down my face. No lie!

They did Sylvia's "Pillow Talk", The Isley Brothers "Don't Let Me Be Lonely Tonight", then closed the set with Patti LaBelle's "You Are My Friend." When they bowed and sashayed off, the crowd blew up. They started hollering for an encore. The girls came back out and did an original piece by Ana Stasia called "Once In My Arms."

When she started singing the music went down low, she was all you could hear for a while. Sept and Pretty came in with the back then both broke down to a solo, Sept was doing her aria then the other two girls came in, the music came up and they got louder then faded out. It was so bad that everybody was froze quiet for about 30 seconds before they all started howling like crazy. The girls bowed and left again. The crowd was going nuts. Dirty ran up to the front of the stage snatched his own wig off, threw it up in the air and passed out right there on the grass.

The girls were so hyper because the crowd was so live. They changed clothes in front of us while laughing and talking like we were their little brothers. They took it off and we packed it up and took it out to the car. Sweater Cap, the promoter came in, paid them, and told them he'd see them at the next gig. After he left she handed us both $5.00 each! Man, she didn't have to give us nothing. We were paid by all of the attention they showed us. My mind was in a whirlpool. Then she asked us what we were doing tomorrow around 4.

Arch told her he was going to be at his grandmother's house. He said that his family spends every Sunday over there. I was free. She told me to meet her at The Dust Bubble at 5.

All of that was 6 years ago. I hadn't written in my journal since then. Now, however, I'm going to finish my discourse.

Chapter 2

ProLong

I was at the Dust bubble at 4:00. I saw a menagerie of people coming and going, mostly moving boxes and bags. There was a couple of fly wheels in front of the building but the oddity was the big dude that kept coming out and going in. He'd put something in this car, take a box of Liquor out of another car. His presence was demanding but I hardly paid any attention to him, my main concern was the arrival of the Heart Attacks.

At 5 till 5, Ana Stasia pulled up with a cat in an off-the-showroom-floor 1976 Cadillac Eldorado. It was triple white with two-inch gangster white walls, convertible of course.

She saw me before she got out of the car, her eyes lit up and she blew me a kiss. She got out of the car only after the dude got out, came to her side and opened her door. She sauntered over to me, kissed my cheek and said,

"Daddy, this is our little sweetheart that I told you about earlier. Bones, this is ProLong, my Daddy."

"What's up Kid? I once knew a cat named Chicken Bones, we called him Bones for short."

"That's my uncle! He used to take me around with him when I was 8 or 9, e'rybody used to call me Lil' Chicken Bones, then they shortened it to Bones!"

"I thought I knew your face. Come here! Hell yeah! Little Chick! Man, your uncle was a good ole dude. We made some long bread together. Look, grab that box out the back seat an' follow me."

Ana Stasia was just smiling at me looking beautiful. The sun was not as bright as her smile. I remember thinking it was like Angel's caresses. When I got the box out she winked at me and walked ahead. I followed the liquid trail of sex that she oozed thinking, "There ain't no doubt about why they call them the Heart Attacks. I was mesmerized by Miss Honey then and even now when I see her from time to time.

When I stepped through the door of the Dust Bubble I was stuck. There wasn't a single unpretentious thing about the red and black decored place. There were red cloths on the tables, the chairs had red backs and red seats. There were two red bars, both with glowing black marble tops. The floor was red and black checked, of course, except for the dance floor which was wooden. There were 4 red doors and one black one which was off to the right away from the kitchen.

I was stunned as to why the place was called the Dust Bubble. There was no dust anywhere in the entire place. There was a section railed off that had 8 leather chairs which looked like large love seats. I assumed the area was the lounge for VIPs. By the kitchen door, in a brass basket there were 50 menus. They were red with black tassels on each one.

"Little Chicken, sit the box on the table an' come with me. --- This is where all of the cleaning materials are kept, brass polish is different than the polish we use for the steel rails over there around the lounge. There's trash bags, rubber gloves, scrub brushes, an' rags, everything you need. The job pays $70 a week if you think you can keep it looking like it looks now. That's $10 a day, it should take you about one or two hours a day, what's up?"

"Bet! I can handle that. What time you want me here e'ry day?"

"Well, Little Chick, every body shows up around 7:30, you need to be here at least two hours before they show so you can make sure everything is tight. You dig?"

"Cool. Do I have to leave before e'rybody shows up?"

"Not really, why you ask?"

"I just ain't never been in a place like this an' I just want to see how e'rybody gets their groove on."

"Look, that third red door is my office, you can hang around as long as you look busy, an' you spend most of your time in there or in the kitchen with Ann Tea an' Muck."

"Who's that?"

"Muck Yoo is our Japanese chef who specializes in French cuisine. You ever eat French food Lil' Cat?"

"No, I only ate Soul food all my life."

"As soon as Muck gets here I'll have him fix you something nice. Go on an'grab a rag an' wipe the rails down. Get the fingerprints off the bars. That black marble was imported from Greece. I got it from an estate sale. A mob cat got iced an' they auctioned his things off."

"I bet you paid big bucks for that."

"Chick, just because we're Black an' live in the ghetto don't mean we can't appreciate the finer things in life. I paid a few ends for it but you gotta be good to yourself man. You ain't good to you, you can't be good to anyone else. ---- See those chairs over there?"

"Yeah."

"They're made outta Italian leather, softer than 16 year old thighs. There's some cats who come here to sit in those seats, they chill out, rap an' drink off of the top shelf. They order Muck's Chateau briand, Loup de Mer, an' Lobster Americaine. They take good care of themselves, because what's life if you don't emphasis your leisure hours? You dig that Baby?"

"That's slick! I diggit!"

"Listen, I'm gone give you this 100 dollar bill. It's your first week's pay plus a $30 sign on bonus. I want you to get you a nice white shirt, some black pants, black flats, thick an' thins and a nice little tie. Get your hair cut, put the rest of your cash up except for about 5 bones.

See, you never want to go anywhere without a taste of scratch in your pocket. An' you don't rush in an' spend that scratch either. You're always lookin' for a thang to do to add to your pocket paper. You see a thang you dig, you save your paper an' cop it. Even if the bread you got'll cop it you don't get it right then. If you need to spend $20, you wait till you got $40, so what you put out you still got. Huh?"

"That's a groove! That's what Chicken used to do, huh? He always kept a B.R."

"Yeah, he knew how to get bank."

"Should I clean up in the clothes you told me to get?"

"Naw baby, you clean up in them Chuck Taylors you wearin' an' them Levis. You keep a set of threads in the back so when you're around the customers you can look fly, cat!"

"I'm gonna jump clean tomorrow after school!"

"That's it, but don't you ever flash your bank roll, nobody should know you're holdin'."

"Just my mother?"

"Nobody Cat! The B.R. is a private matter. If you gone help your momma, do that, but what you got, what you holdin' in your stash ain't nobody's business. An' your stash gotta be so tight that a cat lookin' for an hour can't even find it."

"What if somethin' happens to me?"

"Then it happens with your B.R. safe. ----Take a look around. Never go in that black door, that's my partner, McRotten's, office. Kinda got a bad temper. Killed a man once cause he said dude was too damn ugly to live."

"Pshh!"

"You got that right! What you do every Sunday?"

"I just be layin' low."

"Dig, I know some hustlers like to have their wheels busted every Sunday. Where's your partner?"

"He at his Gran' Mother's on Sundays."

"Hmmm. Okay, dig this. These are big Buck Boys, all of them.

I'll have them give you $10 each. You'll need a washer, a detailer, an' somebody doin' the wheels. You pay a dollar a ride, that leaves you with 7. Don't discuss that with nobody, right?"

"I'm down."

"Awright, you collectin' bread, keepin' count, keepin' track of who did what, makin' sure they doin' their job. If they ain't no good on detail, you give them wheels, no good on wheels, you give them the water, if they ain't no good there you give them the bricks an' you do their job until you replace them. Your math good?"

"Straight A's."

"Slick. You gotta do all this in your head, no paper no pencil. You can't handle that you stick to the cleanin' in here."

"I can handle it."

"You gone be 'round some wires, they gone be doin' their thang. They might get wild, they might not. Can you stay in your place outta the way or are we gone have to get you outta here before they show up?"

"I never get in grown folks business. My mama told me to speak when spoken to an' don't offer up no information. I just wanna be here, if thangs get wild I get ghost. Somebody ask me who been with that girl, I don't know I ain't seen nothin', I don't know nothin'."

"My man! What you eat today?"

"I had two grilled cheese."

"That won't do. You got food at home?"

"Yeah. I was kickin' it with this girl in the neighborhood an' it got late so I rushed some grub so I could get here on time."

"You think you gone like it 'round here Baby Boy?"

"Oh yeah! Can I let a girl help me with the cars?"

"Your call. ---- Hey Muck! Come here. ----- Muck Yoo, this is Little Chicken Bones, you can call him Little Chicken or Bones. He'll be workin' around here, you need anything done in the kitchen or anything, you get Little Chicken to do it, Cool?"

"Okay Boss! Konnichi wa!"

"Little Dude, that means Good day."

"Kan-nichi-wa?"

"Genki desa! That mean fine! What you eat Boss?"

"Hook us up T-bone Perigourdine, sweet potato with tiny peas, hot cross rolls, an' cherry tart. Bring me a white Chianti an' bring bones a 7-up."

That was the biggest steak that I'd ever seen. ProLong (Thomas Ward), took me under his wing and taught me how to enjoy life. He glowed but wasn't extravagant. In fact he was extremely laid back. Ladies loved him for his gentleness and the soft-spoken rap that he put down. When we sat at the table to start our talk Ana Stasia picked up his keys, winked at me and kissed him on the mouth real soft then left. She walked out and I found myself still looking in her direction even after she had shut the door behind herself. ProLong just sat there cool with a smile playing on the corners of his mouth. When I realized that I was still looking at the door I turned around to see that smile. He shook his head and said,

"She'll hurt you kid! Ha, ha, ha!"

"Man, she's pretty as I don't know what."

"Ha, ha, ha, you got a girlfriend?"

"Not really."

"Why not?"

"I don't know, there's these two sisters that me an' my cat be chillin' with named Sugar Roo an'Sugar Ree."

"Which one yours?"

"I be kissin' on both of 'em."

"Oh, little hotties. Naw man, get you a girl that you dig, a little brick house, take her to movies, on walks, talk to her, ---- What's the prettiest sound in the world to a woman?"

"I don't know, the sound of violins?"

"Ha, ha, ha, ha, ha, ha, ha,! Naw Little Chick, the sound of their name, baby. You look her in the eyes, you dig, an' you tell her how good you feel when she's that close to you. You tell her her hair is that thang, her outfit is smokin', see? Be for real though cause you can hook a Honey up with all of that an' if you're playin' a game that you don't understand, you could find yourself under an avalanche cat, you're young, you don't need all that trouble, be good to the Chicken Bone. Make the Honey you choose dig you down to the Soul."

"How you know she's the right one?"

"Shit baby, you'll know that when it's right, look for the signs. You'll know 'em, they're boss."

The wine he ordered came and I watched what he did with it. It was a strange thing to me. He didn't touch it for a while but when he did he swirled it around the glass 7 or 8 times, then he smelled it in his left nostril, then in the right nostril. His first drink he kind of swooshed around his mouth, he said,

"The bouquet, though nebulous, still endures?"

"Huh?"

"Bouquet is the smell of the berry, nebulous means faint, light..."

"So you're sayin' the smell is light but it's still there?"

"Exactly."

"Why do you do that mouth thang?"

"The mouth thing is so I can experience all that the wine has to offer in terms of flavor, what fruit it was made from, what it was aged in. I'm lookin' to see if it's hard, soft, velvety, firm, dry, full, heavy, hearty. I'm lookin' for the balance. No one thing should distinguish itself. This one was aged in oak. Oak gives it a kind of light vanilla thing. I taste the grapes, probably white. This Chianti is from Italy, it's dry and full bodied. But you don't bug with this, you dig? You leave that to the side till it's time. Right now, you learn how to keep gettin' them straight A's an' how to pump your B.R. up. Cool?"

I was hyper on the inside but I was learning how to be cool on the outside like ProLong. I could never tell what was on his mind until he divulged his thoughts, he was like silk pajamas on a satin sheet, just smooth. I'll never forget a thing that he ever said to me. It was all like rhythms out of a Mack manual. Rhythms by which to live comfortably.

He sent me out of the Bubble by 8:30 that first night. People had started showing up by 7 but he kept me out of sight. He said by me coming out periodically taking the trash out, cleaning the ashtrays out on the bar that people would start to get used to seeing me and I would just blend in. But by me being in Pro's office so much they would know that I was tight with the boss and therefore not to be messed with.

The next day at school I wasn't putting on airs, I was just grooving, doing my work and looking around at my classmates. They all seemed smaller, younger that day. I felt like I had graduated but still had to go to grade school.

"You iggin' me?"

"Huh?"

"I asked you what you been up to an' you looked right past me. What's the deal?"

"Sorry, I wasn't iggin' you So-Sho, I was just zonin'!"

"How come you don't ever call me?"

"Girl, you never gave me your number."

"But it's in the book."

"You know that ain't fly."

"Okay, here you go. Call me an' tell me about the show, I heard about it but I couldn't make it."

"Awright. --- That's a nice dress, it's new ain't it?"

"Stop actin' crazy! I been havin' this."

"It's the first time I noticed how good you look in it. I got a little somethin' to do after school, what time you go to bed?"

"About 10, no 10:30."

"I'll call you about 8:45, that cool?"

"My calls stop at 9."

"I better call about 8:30 then."

"Oh, I can stay on the line, I just can't get calls in after 9."

"That works. Catch you later huh?"

That's how things started looking at school. I bought me a new pair of pants and shirt every Friday. I had Arch Terry, and Darlene working for me on Sunday. Arch had been using a lamb shammy on his father's brand new car we ended up buying some of them for our work, I had people asking me for jobs at least three times a day. I took their names and numbers down like a real businessman.

ProLong was right about everybody getting used to me. The bouncer-doorman was called Monkey Paw, he was a man of colossus dimension. When I first saw him, I was in awe to the point of shimmering fear. But with close inspection I found him to be one of the gentlest people that I'd ever met. He was respectful to every lady who crossed the threshold where his enormous graciousness was stationed. He told me that a real man respects womanhood.

After my third week there he had to pistol whoop a cat named Dew Rag. He was a stick up man who tried to put some moves on September, she turned him down. Later he caught her coming into the bubble and pulled his .22 on her. She's so down that she talked him into going inside for a few drinks while they discussed where they would get it on that night. He suggested his car, she told him that she had more class than that and had to go to a hotel room. Rag fell for the okie-doke and came in. As soon as the door was bolted, she whispered to Paw, he busted Dew Rag up with his .38 and threw him in the dumpster.

Dew Rag knew that McRotten would have him done by Sixkill if he would show back up in there, that was one of the very last times I saw him but from the stories, I knew that he was somewhere around. He was obsessed with September. Once I saw him arguing with Shady about Sept. Shady tapped her on the ass when she walked by him. She wasn't mad, in fact she was used to that and most of the cats around here. I heard that she'd turned tricks with a few of the cats who hung around here back in the day.

Sept used to work for Funn. He was a down, pimping hustler. He used to tell me that you always had to know what was going on around you. He told me that women and children could be careless but the men always had to be on their P's and Q's if they wanted to survive. My crew did Funn's Caddy every Sunday. I did his and ProLong's by myself on Wednesdays. Last week ProLong said,

"Hey Chick, make sure you bust them white walls. I went across a pot hole last night an' the tires on the passenger side went down in it. Just hit the red button in the glove box an' the trunk'll open. Everything that you'll need is in there. Use the brillo pads on the walls awright?"

"No Problem"

I popped the trunk but didn't see the brillo so I had to go through a case that was back there. I moved some rags and saw a .22 revolver sitting there. I looked around to see if anyone was looking because I wanted to pick it up, I had never held one. It felt like the toy guns I used to get on Christmas but it had some kind of power, some kind of allure. Pro called my name out and my heart skipped like a girl playing Hop-scotch.

"Chicken Bone?"

"Huh?"

"You find the pads?"

"Yeah!"

"Come on get started, I gotta make a move in about 25 minutes."

"I'll be through by then."

He gave me 12 dollars that day. I didn't have any workers so I kept all of the money. Even though I was buying clothes every Friday I still had a nice bank roll.

I did like I was told. I hid my big end and opened a bank account with $45. I vowed to put $5.00 in the bank every week to give the outward appearance of a tenacious, hard working man. My mother found the book and commented on my ability to stick to my goals. I smiled and thanked her.

Chapter 3

Clubbin'

The first day that I was allowed to be in the club while it was in full swing was April 6, 1976. Ana Stasia, September, and Pretty Penni were supposed to do a set that night. I was excited about that. That was the night that ProLong introduced me to McRotten. He said,

"This here's Chicken Bone's people." He looked at me and said,

"I remember him, that's Jamie's boy." I was shocked, I just said,

"I didn't know you knew my Momma."

"Your father too."

Then he smiled a little smile and kind of back-hand waved me out of his office.

When I was on the other side of the door I heard them both laugh. But I was just glad to get away from there. He had a giant nickel-plated gun on the table that made me as nervous as a dog shitting razor blades! (He knows that every time he shits, he'll cut his ass.) But when I heard the laughter I moved immediately away form the door, I didn't want anybody to think I was a dipper. I knew my place. I was a kid in some real grown folks house. I didn't know why they fell in love with me I only know that they did.

"Hey Honey, come over here would you?"

"Yeah?"

"Sweetness I need you to go down the basement with me to scoop up some bottles of wine. Lord, you are a cutie pie. You ain't scared that I'm gone try to corrupt you in that dark, moist, alcove is you?"

"Ha, ha, ha, ha!"

"Ooh Chile, is that a nervous laugh or what?"

"No, I'm sorry, you got the hair-do, earrings, micro-mini, with Tina Turner legs but you must be pissed......"

"Pissed? Honey what you mean? Pissed about what Chile?"

"For havin' big ass hands!!!

"Ooooh! No you didn't! Ain't that a shame though? Miss Tur's got all of these niceties an' these Go-Rilla hands. I shoulda known that you'd bring Miss a dose of reality. Mercy! You awright! Come on you Demon!"

Miss Tur said that if I had trouble or a problem referring to him as 'her' when talking to other people to use the adverb 'they'. I took the little piece of nothing and stored it. The gratuity that I got from working there was that all of the people in the Bubble told me everything. Miss Tur told me that he started cross-dressing at age 7. He said that he had 5 sisters and started noticing how all of their mannerisms got everybody's attention. He said when he started imitating his sisters everybody would laugh and roll. He became the center of attention and never stopped his little show.

I asked him did people pick on him when he was young. He showed me a cut on his back, he's carried a switchblade ever since. He volunteered the info about his .38 in the car then he smirked and said that it's easier to hide a blade in his mini. I'd seen more guns in the first two months of working the Bubble that I'd seen in my entire life. I asked Miss if he missed being with women, his answer was,

"You can't miss what you can't measure, Sugar!"

"What does that mean?"

"Young Tender, I ain't never been with no woman, how can I miss being with them fishes?"

"Pshh! ---- Why all the wine stored down here an' the liquor stored up stairs?"

"Honey, the liquor hold it's own, it don't sour."

"Sour?"

"Oh yeah! Fluxuatin' temperatures kill wine, make it taste like panther piss."

"Oh, you know, it go limp like a pet...."

"Okay! Okay!"

"Here, get two of them, that there, three of them whites an' that Bordeaux. Honey, they needs them some Thunderbird up in here."

"I had some Thunderbird before."

"Don't you ever do that again!"

"What?"

"Don't drink that gut bucket. That ain't slick. You too young to be all messed up inside. That shit eat your liver. Them crackers want to see a young Black man all messed up in the head like me Baby. That Thunderbird'll take you out the box chile. My ex, Diana..."

"Dirty Diana?"

"Oooh! Honey how you know Dirty? Spill an' don't you jive me!"

"You get too excited, Okay, I met him, well, I didn't meet him. Anyway we were at the Circle. We were in the 2nd row an' Diana was there. He had on hot pants and a wig when ..."

"Wig? The blonde?"

"Yep."

"Oooh!"

"Anyway, when the girls finished their encore dirty ran up to the front of the stage, snatched the wig off, threw it up in the air an' fainted right there in the grass!"

"Lawd hamercy! See? Uh, uh, Chile! That's why I had to go, she'd pull them publicity stunts while we was together an' end up who knows where that night. I be workin' an' she be out whorin' around. Honey, I caught the hoe in bed with a womannnnnn!"

He broke down and real tears broke out! Ask me no questions...! I just stood there with the wine in the carrying case. But as quick as he started, he stopped.

"Chile, see! That bitch still make my make-up run. Severence will kill me if she found out I shed a tear for that tramp. Honey, here you take this ten, an' don't you ever mention this to Sevie if you meet him. Button them lips, Chile!"

"That's hip."

"Don't you jive me!"

"Think we better get back up stairs?"

"Oooh! See! You down by law! McRotten is the real villain. He'll kill me if he think I'm loiterin' on the clock."

"What is that gun he has?"

"Ain't it pretty? All long an' hard an' shiny! Pooh, that's a .357 Magnum. I hear he shot a cat an' the bullet went through him an' kilt three of his boys! Kilt 'em all with one shot! Oooh! Ain't that wicked?"

"Pshh! I heard he's poison!"

"Honey, Poison with a taste for passion! He's with Honi Bunz now, but he done had Ana Stasia, my girl Mini Stirr, Lotta Koochie, shit, I hear he tricked with September an' Fanci at the same time. An' Sweetie, them's only the fishes that works here! Pshh! He won't give Miss the time of day though."

"You tried to get with Rotten?"

"He the boss ain't he? Shit an' I know he got that girl..."

"Shit! You gone drain me of my cash ain't you? I keep runnin' my mouth an' payin' hush money you'll end up with my 'Lack an' I'll be wearin' Chuck Taylors. Here, 5 bones, an' if you tell anybody I told you he sellin' kilos of cocaine I'll cut you boy!"

He pulled his switch blade out so fast and just as swiftly he returned it to its hiding place.

"Damn!"

"Hush your mouth!"

"Sorry!"

"Come on, Chile!"

When we emerged from the lower alcove Shady was sitting at the bar with the dog on his face. I knew I didn't need to be around. I learned how to spot signs. ProLong had told me if I saw anything that looked like trouble to head for his office. As I sat the wine crate down I heard,

"Bitch, where the fuck you been? I been sittin' here thirsty an' you somewhere lolly gaggin'. Now get me a Tanquary before I stomp your ass!"

"Who the fuck you talkin' to?"

Before I could get the door closed Shady Jap-slapped Miss. I saw Monkey Paw spring up and bust Shady in the head with one of his triple large fists. I heard Shady hit the floor but the closed door prevented me from seeing it.

Later I was told that Shady also ended up in the garbage dump. Somebody said Severence, Miss Tur's husband, would kill Shady if he found out about this. Miss broke out in tears and made us all promise not to tell Severence because he would go back to the joint and Miss would 'just die'.

That night is when the stories started floating about Shady. He slung heroin. He would cop bundles, cut them twice and resell them. He raped Lotta Koochie, she went to him to cop a sack of coke and he hit her with some H. She woke up butt naked in an abandoned building. They say the stench is what woke her up. She got a hold of September and swore to her that she was going to kill him as soon as she saw him. Sept talked her out of the confrontation. Dude had killed 4 or 5 cats but Lotta had an atrocious track record and didn't care about Shady's pedigree. Still she held off until her time was clear.

When I talked to Miss that night he said that Shady's little slap kind of turned him on, (he liked rough sex and pain).

I looked around the club, those people came to party. I saw Dead Walkin' Slim, he had on box-toed flats with a brown leisure suit. Big Sally was there with her fast hands. She was one of the best thieves in town. Her and Boostin' Betty ran together. They were in blue and green. Dusty Dave and Nas T. were sitting at the bar both clean as bleached chittlins. Dave had on a two-piece, one-inch, blue striped outfit with a blue satin high boy collar shirt. He had on a Black Tiki with red, black, and green beads. On his left hand he had on a 7 stone diamond cluster pinky ring. His Afro was abut 4 inches long. Nas T. had on a double-breasted suit with black and white Stacy Adams. He had three rings on his right hand, one on his left. He wore his hair in a Superfly perm, down to his shoulders. Little Hootie came in with Molly Body. She had on a light blue Gunny-sack dress with two strings of faux pearls, he was wearing a green Nahru with Black Beetle boots. They both wore three inch Afros.

Lightnin' Quick was there, I saw his hand in Dead Fo' Real's pocket but that was grown folks stuff so I turned my head to it. Damien came in with three yellow hookers and set them off in different directions. He took a seat in the lounge sipping champagne and rapping with Cassanova. I couldn't tell what they were saying but they were laughing big.

About a quarter to 11, I went into ProLong's office to change back into my Levis and Chucks (black) so I could get on home. He asked me if I needed somebody to take me home but I told him that I wanted to walk.

The night was alluring. Inside the club there was a rainbow of women that society calls whores, thieves, and tramps. Those same women surrounded by the walls of the Dust Bubble were Brick houses, Slim Goodies, Foxes and Stars. I knew most of them as mothers, wives, sisters, friends. Outside I stepped three steps from the door and heard,

"Hey you get over here, we been waitin' for you!"

"Me?"

"Yeah, you, punk. We heard you hang out in there. You know we can take your ass down right now to Juvie Hall for bein' in a house of ill repute? Where your Momma at boy?"

"My momma at work."

"Shut up! You been drinkin'?"

"Naw."

"Snortin' a taste?"

"Taste of what?"

"Smart ass bastard. Answer the questions."

"You know McRotten?"

"Yeah, but not good though."

"We hear he kilt some folks a while back. What you know "bout that?"

"I know it's late an' I gotta get up for school tomorrow."

"I oughta..."

"Hold it Dix, listen boy. This is officer Dix an' my name is Darren Jerr. We gone let you go but if we need to ask you some questions, god dammit you better answer or we'll haul your fuckin' ass in so fast it'll make your god damn head swim. You got that, punk?"

"Answer him before I....."

"I hear you. Can I go home now?"

"Get outta my face you disgust me!"

They reminded me of Laurel and Hardy. One fat and one skinny. Both had stupid looks on their faces and their routine wasn't funny. ProLong had warned me about them. They were paid under the table to keep their distance from the club but had a confuting urge to pull up and get snappish with the clientele from time to time. The truth about them was they were just Captain-of-the-shift-ass-kissers. Niggers with badges who wanted to give black folks grief.

Somebody once said that power corrupts, and absolute power corrupts absolutely. That showed in these two clowns. They had their badges, guns, and funny hats and wanted everybody to think they were the cocks-of-the-walk. The truth is they were no more than a standing joke in the streets. Objects of opprobrium in the neighborhood and on the job.

By the time I reached home I was singing Ana Stasia's "*Once in My Arms*". But I was thinking about September and Alexis. When I copped Lexi it was because she reminded me of Sept. She was a foxy little phillie with long straight hair. But there was something about her that called out to me. Something soft, something right. I showed Sept a picture of her and she noticed right away. She said,

"Ooooh! She looks so much like a young me! Awww, Little Chicken you in love with me! I'm flattered!"

"How you know I'm in love with you?"

"Boy, I can see how you stare at me, how you avoid eye contact with me, how you stumble over your words when I pull up on you too quick....Should I go on?"

"Naw. But is that bad though?"

"Naw Little Tommy, as long as you don't try to get in my panties!"

"Woman!! Wait, how you know my name is Thomas?"

"Cause I knew Big Chicken. Boy he was something, he was in love with me too! First time I gave him some, he was so gentle, so smooth. Everybody calls me by the first part of my name, he called me by the last part. He called me Tember. Said I was tall an' proud like an oak tree. He gave me gifts an' perfume, an' never once when he saw me with someone else did he cop a 'tude. He'd smile an' nod an' wait for a hot second when I was alone an' say, "I'll catch you on the flip, Tember." Then he'd walk away all proud an' straight an' tall an' go on back to his hustle."

"Sounds like you was in love with him, Sept."

"Pshh! I thought you knew! You know, I had my gangster an' thangs but he wasn't nothin' like Chicken Bones. My cat was rude compared to Chick, you know? Chick gave me a place to lay down my rules, an' jewels, an' rangs an' thangs. See this piece?---- Chick gave it to me in a small porcelain heart. When he died, I packed the heart up real good in cotton an' stuff so nothin' would ever happen to it. I want you to have this piece."

"Naw, Sept, you need that for the memory."

"Baby, his memory's in my soul. No one ever treated me so delicately. Ever. When I heard about your daddy dyin' an' how Chick hung around your momma to comfort her an' to help with you, I knew then that he was the man that I should a been with all along. He asked me for a chance way back in high school before he started hustlin' an' thangs. Shit, I chose my ganster 'cause he was into all kinds of shit an' it all fascinated me anuff to get wit him, what's her name….?"

"Alexis, I call her Lexi."

"Cute. Buy Lexi something', you know, a little somethin' nice, like a little doo-dad, but give it to her after you take her somewhere an' do somethin' special, not just groovin' off some tunes, you understand?"

"Yep. Sept, can I ask you somethin'?"

"Naw, 'cause you gone ask me why I was a whore. Little Chick, life ain't always easy, Baby. Some women gotta do some shit they ain't never proud of, Chick. Let me tell you this. You do what you can for your mother an' don't give her no lot of trouble. Think everything through. Try not to get hurt an' have to go to the hospital so she'll have to pay all them medical bills, just do what you can to make it easy for her. ------you give her some of your money?"

"Yeah, but she won't take it."

"You buy groceries?"

"No."

"See? You know what y'all eat. You can go to the store an' bring home a couple of bags can't you?"

"I never thought about it like that. But I will. I'll be lookin' for thangs that I can do from now on. I just ain't never thought about that. But I wasn't gone ask you about your business, my Momma taught me not to be pryin' in folks biz. I wanted to ask you, ---you know, ---what do ProLong do to make you happy an' stuff?"

"Aw Chick, he so sweet. He know I love them yellow an' white roses. I be up on stage an' he send a dozen of 'em up there while I'm takin' a bow. He gentle to me not like most pimps. He never put his hands on me. He's not like that at all he's what you would call a Finesse Pimp. His boy Gorgeous George, he hard core gorilla, though. Gorgeous got a girl named Mousie, he beat her ass down on the track. He tell her, "Look up." When she do he knock her right down. He point to the ground an' say, "That way's up." The next day he say, "Look up." Because she look down he knock her down. He point to the sky an' say, "That way's up, bitch!"

"That's crazy!"

"That's the way he keep her off balance. She never know what pleases him so she workin', sellin' her stuff till she 'bout to fallout some days."

"I'll never do that."

"Can't say that, Baby, you might be broke down so far that that's your only way out."

"Naw, I'm savin' every dime I can, gone graduate, get a scholarship an' be somebody."

"Baby, you stand hard on that! How's your grades?"

"I got all A's an' one B+ first quarter. I'll bring the B+ up an' get all A+'s!"

"Look at my Chicken Bone! Boy, you graduate an' me an' the girls gone sing at the ceremony."

"For real?"

"Bank on that, Kid!"

I walked around the quiet, empty house just looking. I walked into Jamie's room. Everything was so neat, carefully placed, meticulous, significant. I thought of my mother differently that day. I thought of how organized her thoughts were, how caring she was, even for the smallest of things.

She had a potpourri jar in the corner where I always saw the sun shining. I could smell the scent of roses and orange lying informally in the air. I realized that I was looking at a number of items that she placed a lot of emphasis on. A small picture of my father in a heart-shaped frame sat next to a bottle of perfume that she dabs on from time to time. I knew then that when she dabs on that scent and feels good about herself my father is a faction of those feelings.

The one picture that Momma had of Chick was on the living room wall. I walked out to look at it.

Big Chicken was a good dude. He just stepped up when daddy died. He would take me to the park and I didn't even have to ask him. He bought Momma daisies in a vase. He made her laugh, that big laugh, like she used to share with Daddy. Once I saw her cry and put her head on Chick's shoulder. He looked past her to me, and his silent lips said, "She'll be okay." Then he smiled to me to let me know that everything was cool.

He took me around a lot of people who remind me of the folks that I see in the Bubble. He took me in some places but there were some spots that he absolutely wouldn't allow me to enter. Most of the time he would leave me outside with a lady, sometimes with a man, but never for long. He wouldn't go in and forget me, ever. Whoever he left me with would talk to me like I was their son. They would ask me things like do I remember to say my prayers at night, do I brush after meals, say thank you and please.

I know my momma loved Big Chick and would love to have something that belonged to him. She would be home in nearly two hours, she'd fix herself something light to eat then go to sleep. She likes my omelets. I cook them with 3 cheeses, and Kielbasa sausage. Then I grate some more cheese, dice some green peppers and sprinkle that across the top. I knew she'd be coming through the door at 1:05 so I started some toast at 1:03. by the time she came through the door I had the eggs cracked, the peppers and cheese ready and had the Stevie Wonder "Inner Visions" on. She came in on "don't you worry about a thing."

"Tommy, Baby, what you doin' up?"

"Look at you! Work them fingers down to the bones and you still got time to worry 'bout your man-son. Give me them bags an' sit down right there."

"Boy, what you up to? Lawd! You got some gal pregnant?"

"You so silly! I ain't even went to the bottom of the ninth!"

"Ooh! But..."

"But nothin'. Smell, tell me what that is."

"Ooh, Chile, you cookin' your Gran' momma's Creole omelet! Come here, look at me in the eyes, tell me what's up."

"Momma, I love you. I just wanted to sit down with you for ten minutes an' listen to you talk. Tell me 'bout your day or night."

"Baby, if I'm given ten minutes, I'd rather listen to you talk about your day."

"Mamma…."

"No. You!"

"Okay, I got a main pain named Alexis, I call her Lexi. I got a hundred in math, English an' science. Went to work today, polished some brass an' thought about you. Your turn!"

"That's not talkin' that's a book report. Okay, I had kind of a hard day, got a bill for the lights, it's $75. I can't put that in my budget this week so I'll have to get it paid on an' then paid off. I asked my boss for a raise, he turned me down. So I had to worry 'bout that…."

"Okay, okay, that's not quite what I had in mind either. Don't trip off of that. Eat. What you want to drink?"

"Juice."

"Cool. Now you chill, I'll be right back."

"You ain't eatin'?"

"Uh huh! Chill."

I went to my room, I'd already taken $200 out of my stash, it wasn't one third of what I had put up. ProLong said if I spend 10, I better have 10 left.

"Hey, gorgeous, when you drink the juice, open this."

"What is it?"

"Who knows?"

"Come on!"

"Nope, juice first!"

"Okay, that's the juice!"

"Go ahead."

"Boy!! This is $200! What…?"

"Take a chill pill! I saved it from my job."

"But your bank book says $115."

"How you know that?"

"I saw it when I was……."

"..Cleanin'. I know! Mamma, I saved it for an emergency like this. An' I'm beggin' you to take it. Pay the bill an' buy yourself a new dress."

"Lord chile, you are growin' up! Let me look at you."

"Look at you! All sensitive! Momma, you raised me right. You, Daddy, an' Big Chick. Y'all taught me to be a man for the woman in my life. That's you! Dig, Momma, you talk about Daddy but you don't talk about Big Chicken much, why?"

"Honey, it's hard to talk about the death of loved ones. One death is enough."

"But Mamma, he stepped up. How you feel about Unc?"

"Baby, he was a special person. He loved your Daddy an' would have done anything in the world for you. He vowed to raise you like you was his own."

"How come you don't have any pictures of him but that one?"

"Chicken didn't like to take pictures. He thought they would be the thang that would take him down. He said maybe somebody would be able to identify him for some dirt that he done in the past."

"Pshhh! ---- Hold on ma. -------Here you go."

"What's in the box?"

"Open it!"

"You're full of 'em tonight!----- Oh that's beautiful!!! That must have cost you a fortune. Uh, uh, Baby no…"

"Mamma, it's from Big Chicken."

"What?"

"Chick gave it to a woman…"

"What woman?"

"Chill Jamie! Chick gave it to a woman named September…"

"September?"

"Momma…"

"Okay, tell your story."

"He gave this piece to a girl named Sept he was in love with. The first time I met her she was on her way to work. She sings with a band. Me an' Arch met her an' she told us she was singin' at the Circle so we went. When we saw her there she had us carryin' her bags, outfits and stuff an' she got me this job. She remembers me from bein' with Big Chicken. We talked about him for a long time then she gave me this, said she wanted me to give it to you cause she knows how Chick loved you."

"That's a big story, I don't know what to say big man. It ain't nothin' like the Math-English thing!"

"Say you love it."

"I do. But I love you a thousand times more!"

"Good, then e'rything's like I planned!"

"But what about …?"

"Lexi? You'll meet her Saturday afternoon. We're goin' to the mall to the movie."

"My baby's growin' up."

"But not too grown to sit on your lap an' kiss you goodnight!"

"Honey, there's somethin' I wanna talk to you about."

"Go!"

"I met a man, I think he's nice, he an' I like each other --- a lot…"

"When were you gonna tell me?"

"When I thought you could handle it. I know you can now. We talked, he wants to move in. But first he wants to meet you an' talk to you."

"I'm down, when?"

"How 'bout Saturday?"

"That's hip. I'll bring Lexi, you can check her out an' I can check-out …."

"Paul."

"I'll check Paul out, we'll discuss them later, alone. Bet?"

"Bet! Now go to bed. I'll get the dishes."

"I love you , Ma!"
"I love you more!"
"No, I love you more! More! More!"
"I love you all the way to Heaven's door!"
"Night."

Chapter 4

Funn

Funn was one of the VIP's at the Bubble. A hustler, pimp, dope mover. I could lay his story down next to others of his caliber, run down his pedigree by contradistinction, and it would only prove that he was one up in his game. Funn was a Stacy Adams man. I've seen him in several different two-toned Stacys. He had the black shoe with the white, red, and yellow on them. Every time he had on the tones his silk or satin shirt would match the second color of the shoe. Then he had the high-top Stacys in gray, black, an' brown.

Funn had some of the finest rags that were ever tailor made. He had one cream, double-breasted, in-striped piece. Then a red three-piece that he wore with a gold pocket watch and chain. It hung like a 'W' across the two vest pockets and ran through the third button hole of the vest. When he had this on he checked the watch often, it's not like he was in a hurry to go somewhere on time, it was just a part of his show. He had a white double-breasted trey that the silk shirts accentuated. Funn was the inventor of conspicuous consumption. He'd come in during the full dinner hours and order the house. Sometimes he'd bring in 3 or 4 of his girls, feed them all well and then set them off on the track.

He'd start with something like deviled crabs, shrimp curry, soft shelled crabs with almonds, Billi Bi, or black bean soup. Then he'd have Lobster Americaine, Chateau Briand, Filet Mignon, or Frog legs Provencale. I've seen him order Filet de Perron la Gourdine, Meat loaf Oriental and oh, yeah! Quenelles de Brocket Lyonnaise. I loved how he high-sided! He'd eat his meal slow and cool, sipping Chianti, Merlot, Bordeaux, Chardonnay, or Chablis.

Since I've been working there I've seen him order everything on the menu except "Thank You!"

One time he ordered Filet de Muck Yoo. Muck came out of the back speaking Japanese real fast and waving his cleaver. All of Funn's girls broke out laughing but Funn just threw both hands up like he was holding Muck off and said, "English, muthafucka, English!" It was funny though. Funn was the only one who could get under Muck's skin. But quiet as it's kept I think that Muck loved it when Funn knuckled him like that. Funn must have loved it as much, he did it at least once every time the clock struck twelve.

Muck had a protégé we called Ann Tea, Aintee when you say it fast. Ann could cook up that Soul Food and was a hellava baker! She'd bake Rum pie, Rum Bumble with cream, sprinkled with toasted almond, Lemon Cream Meringue, Chocolate Angel Pie, Apple Crumb Pie, Sherry Soufflé, Macaroon Soufflé, and her famous Tropical Gingerbread. Funn had her bake every one of these two at a time. He and his "Havin' big-big fun!" crew would eat one and the other he would take with him. They say that he takes the second one to his mother.

He had style, once two of his girls, Lotta Koochie an' Wee Gee, (Gee Gee's twin) got into an argument at the table. He just picked up his spoon and tapped the side of his wine glass. Both of the women snapped to attention. They realized what they had done and just looked at each other with caring sympathy as they sat there still. I couldn't read anything on his face, no disgust, no frown. He put the spoon down, sat back in his seat. His eyes went from Lotta to Wee Gee at the same time he was rubbing the two karat diamond ring that he wore on his right had. One at a time they picked up their drinks, inhaled them and dismissed themselves. They walked out of the door together.

Funn said something so low that only the ladies, Fanci, Gee Gee, and Dee Lux, at his table could hear him. They all laughed as if the thing that had recently transpired was now abdicated. That's the way he was. Everything about him was portentous to me, raped in a veil. He was one of the hardest people for me to read.

ProLong would sit with me behind his two way mirror and point people out and ask me what they were thinking, what would they do next or what they did for a hustle. What I could say about Funn was diminutive. I could only generalize. He was gregarious, pernicious, unselfish and had a sense of humor. His character had few visible impediments. He was unrestricted in his movements. But I could never tell if he was sad, mad, or glad. His feelings were like a private thing to him. His composure was intact even at times that I would have thought to be moments of adversity.

One Sunday he was getting his Caddy detailed by my crew, I had Arch, Terry tornado,

and LaLa with me. Funn and Dee Lux were off to the side, low-talking, close-talking. All anyone could hear was periodic laughter. Real laughter. Before Funn had gotten out of the car I saw him put a .22 revolver in his pocket that he took out of the glove compartment. He had on a black leather, maxi coat with a sable collar. I know how easily the gun slid into his pocket and with the coat on it was impossible to know he had it. He was standing next to the building when Shady pulled up in his Chevy Impala. He parked his car aslant, jumped out and rushed up to them.

"Your bitch owe me a hunnit bones."

"You talkin' to me?"

"damn right!"

"You owe him?"

"I don't owe nobody but you. I don't pay nobody but you."

"So what you talkin' 'bout partner?"

"I was with that hoe last night, gave her a hunnit, shot a piece an' when I come out the nod the bitch gone."

"You paid for what you got cat, a baby sitter to watch you nod. You pay by the hour not the act, dude."

That's when he slid his hand into his pocket.

"Fuck that. I'll…."

"You'll take a step back, turn around an' get in your car an' enjoy another sun set. Beyond that ain't nothin' guaranteed."

"Bitch" Came out of his mouth almost inaudibly. Still, he turned on his heals, got in his car and left.

That's when I heard Funn say something shocking I'd never heard escape his cool,

"That's his last time up in my face."

He didn't look upset, he wasn't frowning. He just said it. He got close to Dee's ear and she laughed again.

I can't figure out what's wrong with Shady. I heard that he took pussy from Lotta. I think now that was what he meant when he said that. Shady had kept crossing him. But Shady crossed everybody.

Yesterday I heard that Severence was finally hip to what went down between Shady and Miss. They say he went ballistic at the apartment, he shot up the couch, Miss said he "kilt the couch!" Everyone says that Miss snatched his wig off, dived on the floor in front of the door and begged Severence not to go out the door because if he left he would never come back. That's why he shot up the couch. They say they had a wild sexcapade right there on the floor. The neighbors who heard the shots ran to the door and all they could hear was inarticulate words of passion (for no less than an hour).

The next day (Monday) Miss came to the Bubble eupeptic and energetic, he was singing "Man of My Dreams" and drinking Cafe Latte instead of his usual Gin Screw. I asked him what was up cause I'd never seen that side of him. His words were,

"Chick, one day you gone find somebody you love so much that you gone be able to feel them move right inside of you. You'll wanna eat, drink, an' sleep that person, an' when you do get that lucky you'll think that you done died an' went to Heaven. An' if I see you on that day I'll know it cause you'll be singin' just like me, Chile!"

"So this is what you call Love?"

"Honey, I mean!"

Chapter 5

B. Down

Saturday couldn't get here quick enough, I was in a hurry for my Mother to meet my Honey date.

Alexis was a cheerleader, that made all the cats on the B-ball team think they could have her, I know they all wanted her but I don't ever sweat that. She told me they just talk vulgar and grab their nuts all the time. She says they think that turns all the girls on. She said she first started digging me when she got wind of the show at the Circle. Then she got to know me and started digging how I handled myself.

Lexi's ice cold! She likes to read poetry and a lot of love stories. She recited Nikki Giovanni's "Revolutionary Dreams" for me. Baby got all the way into it like she was Nikki. That's what made me want to get into poetry heavy. Then I got into Shakespeare. Man, I didn't know what he was talking about. Then I dug my ear in real deep, when I heard him saying 'cuz' and 'bro' I realized that he wasn't all that bad. Then I got into the work. I realized that most people would watch the Hatfields and the McCoy's but wouldn't read Romeo and Juliet but they were the same story, one is just posh and the other is putz. I started reading a lot of his work then started to look for Black poets. I found some Dunbar, W.E.B., Booker T., then I found me some J. Weldon Johnson. Then some where along the way I found me some Gil Scot-

Heron. He was the closest thing to me at the time. I recited his, "When the Revolution Comes" to Lex and she flipped. I did it for her on the way to meet Momma and Paul.

"Momma!? Where you at Jamie?"

"Here I am, what you hollerin' about? Oh! Who is this?"

"Momma, this is Alexis, Lexi, this is the only woman that I've ever loved beside you!"

"You so crazy! Nice to meet you Mrs. Baker."

"Uh, uh, Honey you either call me Momma or Jamie, Mrs. Baker is his grandmother's name!"

"Okay, Momma."

"Momma, where's Paul?"

"Oh, Honey, he'll be right back, he went to get some ice cream. We're havin' Apple Crumb a la mode. Now you run on in to your room an' do what ever you be doin' in there while me an' Lexi do some girl talkin'."

"There y'all go! Lex, don't let her show you them ugly baby pictures!"

"My baby was not ugly!"

"Aw Lord! She'll get sentimental if I don't split! I'm bailin'!"

"Girl, how you put up with him?"

"He's so cool! Not like the other dudes."

"How's that?"

"There's this one boy at school who keep tryin' to get with me, every time he ask me for a chance an' I turn him down he grab his stuff an' say, "You don't know what you missin'!" That makes me so mad! They think just because I'm a cheerleader that they can say what they want to me. But Tommy……."

"Tommy? I'm surprised you call him that an' not Chicken or Bones."

"He told me you're the only one who calls him Tommy so I started callin' him that too. I think he likes it better than Bones."

"Naw, Honey he just likes you. He's a good son, girl, an' he'll look out for you, all you gotta do when you find that type of man is be true. He'll take care of you to the end. He takes after his father. He rescued me from a bad situation and stayed with me, in love, till the day he died."

"Tommy told me about the accident."

"I'm surprised, then again I'm not. He don't talk about death much. I know he misses his father but he's dealt with it so well. -------- Hey! Look who's here! Paul, come here Honey. Tommy, come here Baby!"

"What's up momma…? B. Down!"

"Bones!"

"What! You two know each other?"

"Momma, he the D Jay over there where I work!"

"At the Dust Bubble?"

"Yeah."

"You ain't never been in there have you?"

"Momma you trippin'!"

"Uh, uh! Not while they doin' they thang?"

"Pshhhhh!"

"Boy!"

"Momma, why you flippin'?"

"They do drugs in there. Be shootin' …."

"Momma, e'rybody in there looks out for me like Big Chicken did. Matter of fact most of them knew him. Where you think I know September from?"

"You said she sung at the park."

"She did, but she works at the Bubble."

"Paul!!?"

"Honey, he's right, everybody in there looks out for him. They all know he's ProLong's cat….."

"Kenny Edwards?"

"Yeah."

"Oh God! That explains the money!"

"No it don't!"

"Hush Boy!"

"Naw Momma, cause it ain't nothin' like you think it is. I clean, polish, wax. An' if anything looks sticky, I go to ProLong's office."

"Sticky?"

"You know, uh an argument or disagreement."

"Yeah, right. – Boy!….."

"Hold on Momma, I thought you trusted me."

"I do."

"Then chill out an' turn that bird over! Your dinner turnin' while you trippin'.

I go to work, I get my pay, I stay outta the way. I love you Momma. B. down's my cat, he won't let anything happen to me, won't let me get into anything that you wouldn't let me get tied up with…. Down, this is Lexi."

"Paul, you better watch out for him real good an' if anything gets rough you get him out an' don't let him come back. What about the police?"

"They seen me there."

"Seen you there?"

"They know I'm the trash boy an' yeah they see me there, I wash cars on Sunday. E'rybody seen me there once or twice, e'ry Sunday them dudes Dix an' Darren Jerr come around mean muggin' e'rybody, but they just ask me, "What you doin' hangin' round these folks?" I say, "I'm just tryin' to make an honest buck." They say, "You better stay honest or we bust your ass."

"They put they hands on you?"

"Naw, they ain't got no reason. You come around on Sunday, you'll see. Down, you bring her…."

"Oh no! She don't like that place, cat! But Jamie, ain't nothin' gone happen to Bones. Like I say, he's ProLong's cat, treat him like he flesh an' bones. Even that queer ass Miss Turr treat him like family. Bones the only male that I ever seen him with, besides Ann Tea's son, that he don't talk that gay shit to. I peep them talkin' one day so I ease up on him to see if he tryin' to push up on Bones. But he trip me out, he givin' Bones advice. He sayin', Keep your grades up an' stay outta trouble an' you can get your Momma outta here an' in a house on the hill where she don't have to work long hours.

"---Hi Lexi!!!!" She smiled and waved.

"He said that?"

"Pshh! He surprised me, girl! I ain't never hear him give real advice! An' Big ass Monkey Paw act like he all hard, an' Bones come around an' he be grinnin' an' noddin' his head like he approve."

Momma looked at me with her water eyes, I could tell she was proud of me. She once told me that a man can be measured by his friends more than the amount of approval or disapproval he gets from people around.

My Mother's the type of person who works too hard and too long to have to be worrying about me. I'm the only somebody she got and she got to be able to trust me. She don't have to tell me to get good grades, go to school on time, clean my room, not to hang out with thugs. I do all of those things because when we think of each other and when we pass in the halls we do so in a light and airy breeze. When she has things on her mind, we can try to work on them together. We talk things out. If I'm going through a tough time she's there. Home is our haven and I will never bring discordance here. Arch tried to talk me into bringing the Sugar girls there once while Jamie was at work but I talked him down. Some of the cats at school do things because everybody else does. I refuse to go down like that. I'll stay to my self first. I don't care what they say. Besides that I can fight. Daddy and big Chick taught me to throw them knuckles. I taught me how to avoid all of that mess.

My girl is tight though, she's like me in a lot of ways. She doesn't believe in having sex right now. We both think we're too young. Oh, we kiss and grind, she even showed me all of her stuff! She promised me when I got old enough she would let me take her cherry. That filled me up with pride. I thought about how we would be, neither of us knowing anything about sex then getting down. I thought about sex but I don't sweat it. I love Lexi not Sexi.

We talk about everything, our families, school, (Mrs. Brook's tacky wig!), what we want to do later in life. She wants to be a doctor. Think of that! A Black female doctor. I guess by the time we get out of school and college they might have one in the United States, If nothing else, the way them boys keep getting hurt and killed over there in Nam, they could use some extra doctors, no matter what color.

I want to be a writer, that's why I jot down all of these things that have happened in my life. I know I have to get started now so by then I can look back at these journals and have a few records of my past experiences. By the time I learn how to write for real I'll have a ton of old stuff I can go back to and laugh at.

I'm going to write Lexi's bio when she becomes a doctor but for now I'll just write her a few poems and more of those sweet love letters that she adores. It's easy to write to her, for her. I don't have to worry about syntax or diction. I just write from the heart. I learned that from ProLong. I talk to her about how I feel when she's near, and most importantly how I feel when we're apart.

Sometimes when I scribe to her I slip my letters in her locker, in her books. Always she finds them then finds me. One bright canary yellow envelope was found in her locker, it (Canary is her favorite) prompted her to find me immediately. She pulled up on me in the hall by the office. She ran up to me and kissed me in the mouth in front of everyone! Lucky for me there was no staff in the hallway. But I heard rumors about it all day. It got way out of hand. They said we were kissing, swapping spit, and grinding all up side of the wall. Immaturity has no boundaries neither does the snow-ball-going-ace-boon, Tralla, we looked at each other and laughed. She was Lexi's ace but she could lie like a dog. We knew that most of the things that came out of her mouth had to be scrutinized and you'd end up subtracting 3 or 4 from them.

Tralla was a cute little, chunky girl with big, big jokes, and bigger gossip. Her thing was, "Girl, I was sittin' under the grapevine an' the sweetest cherries fell into my lap. You know such-an' such is doin' so-an'-so? If I'm lyin', girl, I'm flyin'!" Sometimes I'd take her by the shoulders and turn her around. She'd go, "What you doin', boy!?" I'd say, "lookin' for your wings."

She was having sex at least two or three times a week and always tried to push me and Lex into getting it on. When she did Lex would just dismiss her and the two of us would laugh about the mess that Tralla had been telling us that day. Lexi would tell her,

"Girl, that 's too heavy! Hustle the theory to somebody who's tryin' to hear it! Now get ta' steppin'!"

"I'll catch y'all on the cool side! Bones, you got my number?"

"Girl, I'll scratch your eyes out!"

"Ha, ha, ha! You know I don't want yours. I'd have too much to teach him! He couldn't comprehend it but he do have potential!"

"Keep on truckin'!"

Like I said, she's cute but I couldn't put up with that kind of girl as my lady. She goes with Christmas Tree but she'll fuck anybody with a car. Some 10th and 11th graders have picked her up while was walking with me and Lexi. She'll be in her tight hip-huggers strutting her stuff. And get snatched right up. She had a pair of jellies for every outfit that she had. But when she wore her micro-minis and tube tops she'd wear her white go-go boots or her box-toed platforms.

Her hair changed everyday, Afro puffs, Afro, hot-combed into a fall, braided and beaded, dyed and dolled. When she wore the fall she'd sling her head back and forth, side to side making sure that her hair slung all over the place. She wore it parted down the middle with the left side pushed back over her ear, the right side fell loosely over her cyc. Tralla had a way when she talked to you. She'd laugh and her hand would find its way to your person. On you shoulder, your arm, your back, your face. She's 'accidentally' brushed my Johnson before. I said, "Hey!" She said, "Sorry, it was just a accident!" This girl was raw, hotter than bad breath but she was Lexi's cat and I didn't try to come between that.

Lex wanted to know what I thought about Tralla hangin' with us when we go places. And what I thought about her hanging out with her girl. I said y'all tight, grew up together, what would I say? I said, y'all cool so that 's cool with me. The girl is wild like cowboy movies but she's your cat. You like it, I love it. She said she was glad I could over look Tralla because she was her best friend and the only one who she trusted completely.

I broke it down like Gorgeous George told me when I asked him how come he didn't bring his woman into the Bubble. (Miss Turr told me that she was so beautiful that she could make him change his constitution!) Gorgeous said, "When you're in a din of low-lifes makin' paper, you get paid and' leave your real life separate from that. Bring her here an' every dick an' his hoe'll be at yours if she's fine. You don't even bring your most trusted friend around your woman all the time, cause just like you fell in love wit her he will too, or he'll fall in lust. Shit, how could he not? Y'all laughin' havin' a good time. He's swimmin' in her beauty as much as you. He figure he's entitled to her.

I told her that's why me and Arch only hang tight when she's not around because the time we have is ours. If Arch wants to hang he'll have to wait till I break. I don't care if we're just discussing math, he'll have to take a pause for my cause. She said, "But Baby, she ain't like that." Pshhhh! I didn't tell her about the accidents though. That wouldn't be cool. I had her promise me that she would allow Tralla to spend as less time with us as possible, I told her she could hang out with her any time, any where though. She was in agreement with that arrangement.

Chapter 6

Gorgeous George

Once ProLong had me looking through the 'Voyeur Glass'. The Bubble was full of regulars and a slew of party people that I had never seen. The whole point to the 'game' had eluded me so I asked him,

"Why do you like guessing at these people?"

"Ha, ha, ha! Little Chicken Bone! When you see anybody walk past that mirror, I already know 99% of their life story. This game ain't for me it's for you."

"Me! Why?"

"Cause Baby, if you can look at a person an' know them before they know you, then you one up on them. Look at dude there. What you see?"

"I see his eyes coverin' e'ry inch of the club, he done checked e'rybody out at least twice."

"What he gone do?"

"Pshh! I ain't hip."

"Awright, see that cat in the lime green jumpsuit with the orange platforms?"

"Yeah."

"He been buyin' liquor all night so that means that he got some kind of bank cause every drink has come off the top shelf. Your cat with the rovin' eyes, he's a drifter. He's lookin' for spenders so he can work his show on 'em an' make that B.R. float right into his lap. In the next few minutes he's gone ease up on Lime Green. He let Lime suck down a gallon so when he pulls up his shit sounds like gravy. Look! Look!"

"Man, that's busted! He right over there talkin' stuff, hands wavin', head an' shoulders rockin'!"

"He workin' that show. What about that girl there?"

"I would say booster or hoe. No wait, I'll definitely say hoe."

"Why?"

"She dressin' that . When you look out there your eyes' keep fallin' on her. If she was a booster she wouldn't want to be seen. Hoe money counts on bein' seen."

"You gettin' good but she boost by day, hoe by night."

"Damn!"

"Watch your mouth. Ha, ha, ha! Okay, dude with the black maxi."

"He done been in the restroom at least 6 times. I seen him talkin' to e'rybody that I seen blowin', so he the powder man."

"What else?"

"He's conservative, he don't wear a lot of rangs an' thangs, he don't like to draw attention to hisself, He look like a fox, real slick, real smooth. 9 outta 10 times he carry one of them .357's that McRotten got on his desk."

"Good call, he sold that to Mc. What else?"

"He drinkin' either orange juice or screwdriver…"

"Juice…"

"Okay, he ain't tryin' to get loaded an' he got the powder an' he ain't usin'..."

"Why you say that?"

"Cause he came out of the restroom with Lime Green, dude in the red pants, an' the cat in the paisley high boy. All three of them keep wipin' their noses an' movin' around fast an' talkin' up a storm. He ain't even touched his nose an' he's real mellow, like low key."

"My dude! His name's Gorgeous George, he's a gambler, dealer, an' second story man." I asked what that was.

"A cat who does robberies. A cat burglar."

"Oh, I get it, he climbs up an' goes in the second story."

"Yeah, like that. Couldn't see that, huh?"

"Don't he have to case the place for a while, make sure e'rybody out of his way before he go in?"

"That's why he stay so cool, he don't drink, smoke, or do girl when he gone do a job. He likes to come round spots where there's a hundred things goin' on. He can tell you every thing about everybody. Tomorrow, when he's all the way cross town, he can tell you about this whole spot. He can tell you where cats were standin', where they spent most of their time at, and probably what they were drinkin'."

"He do all that so he can stay up on all the stuff goin' on around him when he's on a job?"

"Yeah. Now what does that say about him?"

"Even though he a hustler...."

"No, just because he a hustler don't mean he ain't a careful professional. Cat when you do a thing, you do it all the way. Right to the roof!"

"But you part owner of this place, how come you don't own it?"

"This place ain't nothing. It's like my office. Check it out, Long Greene's a gambler, that's that dude there. An' he's cold with it. But durin' the day he works at the Electric Company. Electricity's his front. That's what he wants everybody to see. An' when he shows up with a 'Lack nobody trips, no body wonder where he got it."

"So, is this your front....?"

"See that girl over there? What's her story?"

"Her man. Her man left her, ran off with her sister, took her stereo. ----She caught him in her, no, her in his bed. Now she's drinkin' to forget about him an' her."

"Damn, you see all that in her face?"

"Nope! She told me! You ain't the only one around here who knows people."

"I see!"

That's what first piqued my interest in second story conduct, then in George. I wanted to write about something that he does so I started with what was obvious before I decided to ask him some questions. The name was easy, he's an octoroon, quadroon, mulatto. His father's an octoroon, his mother, of course, is one fourth African. She has German-Irish in her. He came out as light as the Germans in his family line. If his hair wasn't a large black Afro nobody would have believed he was black.

About 2 months after I first saw him through the voyeur glass I started seeing him in the Bubble more regularly. He mostly drank Chardonnay with his meals. He ate here a lot but only ordered half servings of his meals. He ate all of the light meals like Shrimp Canapé aurum, Oyster Bisque and Crab Bisque. He ate shrimp cutlets with a taste of Ann Tea's apple crumble or huckleberry pie. Most men his size ate twice what he ate, at least.

He would have me running back and forth to the kitchen with his orders. Even though he ordered half he always paid the full price and tipped each time I made a run. Sometimes I'd make $20 a night just waiting on him alone. One time he invited me to sit down and eat a slice of crumb bumble with him. Even the wine that he drank didn't make him change like I thought wine should. He was still poised, he talked in low tones, like what he said didn't have anything to do with anyone else but me and him.

"So Little Man, what you doin' in here for real? You tryin' to get in the game?"

"Naw, I just do some odd jobs around here an' pick up a little scratch. My Momma works an' I like to try to help out whenever I can."

"So you can't find a job at McDonald's?"

"Too young."

"How you get here?"

"I met September, Ana Stasia, an' Pretty Penni an' they had me carryin' their bags at the show they did an' they asked me to help out with the trash here."

"What about school?"

"I'm outta here by nine then home an' bed. I get straight A's."

"That's slick. A young Black brother needs to work hard in school. Get them grades right, make 'em give you a scholarship. What grade you in?"

"I'll be in the ninth next year."

"8th grade an' in a Pit of Despair. Boy, you need to be hangin' out with kids your age. With a little Cutie Pie."

"I do hang out with people my age, we wash the cars in the back on Sundays."

"Oh yeah, I heard about the crew hookin' up the wheels. How long you plannin' on workin' here?"

"I don't know, why?"

"Cause man, when you're around a cat who sells perfume, even if you don't sell it you still start smellin' like his scents. You start hangin' with a cat who shovels shit for a livin' you will smell like shit, boy."

"You sayin' if I stay here long I'll end up doin' what most of these people do?"

"That's right kid. You are smart!"

"I wouldn't do a second story job."

"What?"

"I couldn't stand the height. Then I couldn't boost cause I wouldn't know where to stash the loot, plus I'd shake when I came past the security. I couldn't sell dope cause drugs had something to do with my father an' uncle's deaths."

"How so?"

"A cat was high on H. Drivin' a stolen car, hit my father an' killed him. Then my uncle was killed by a fiend tryin' to get coke money. Dude shot my uncle three times in the head, then three times in the heart an' left him face down on Five."

"Fifth Street? Chicken Bones was your people?"

"Yeah."

"Aw Shit! That's why they call you Little Chick. I thought it implied that you had game like Chick or something. I was cool with your people. Your daddy was Kwan Baker. Yeah, he was an awright cat. Damn, I remember when both of 'em died. An' you're right, drugs was the bottom line to both deaths. ------ You're Jamie's boy."

"How come e'rybody knows my mother an' father?"

"Your mamma used to hang out, you know, dance, not workin' girl or nothin'. She liked to laugh a lot, party. One night a cat was getting' rough with her, your daddy always liked her, but she was just a square, you know? So dude got to pushin' Jamie around an' then he slapped her. Kwan beat dude till he was almost dead. Dude was a piece of shit so when the police came an' started questionin' people about what happened they couldn't get a thing. They dropped the case I guess. Your father an' mother got married an' had you."

"Dang, that's not how the story went, well, it goes like that but I guess some of it's been left out."

"It's okay, you were young, you were supposed to get the watered down version."

"Why you give it to me straight?"

"Cause I know who you are, an' too many of your people got trampled down an' trapped in the jaws of game. Now you all up in here. Just don't get your feet wet. First it's the C., then the A., then U.G.H.T."

I asked him about the second story thing. I told him I was trying to be a writer and I wanted to write something about it in my journal.

He told me a cat with that calling had to be agile, dexterous, patient, an' has to have nutts. He told me how he got wind of a doctor who moved dirty money for some big heroin dealers. He kept the paper in a safe in his penthouse apartment 25 stories above the city. He wore his blonde wig the night he did the job. He took the service elevator up to the roof, dropped his rope, descended the side of the building.

One billion lights below bid him ill consequence. When he reached his destination his complaint was, "This ass hole locked the door. Who the shit locks a terrace door 25 stories above the city?" He had to cut the window to gain access to the apartment. The doctor was out on the lake with some of his clients, no doubt discussing the extralegal movement of more dirt-dollars. George had the safe opened within 30 seconds of trying, seconds after that he was burned by a booby trap. A two-shot derringer was concealed inside of the strongbox with a 30 second delay.

That was the first time he had been bitten by a trap. He was unloading Doc's cash when the gun went off. The hot lead erupted through the black velvet that lined the walls of the cash box. Accredited to his agility, after the first bullet hit his left shoulder, he evaded the second loud blast.

Ignoring the pain he unloaded the money into his sac while a Loud-Mouth alarm blared. He escaped using a de-elevator device connected to his climbing rope. With this he jumped off of the side of the building, 15 floors later he stopped over the balcony of one of the luxury suites. The rope disengaged from above after de-elevation was complete. He released the harness and the rig fell easily to his feet. He gathered his gear, slid the door open and entered with stealth. No one was in. He quickly went to work cleaning the wound and patching it. He went to the closet and found a suit that fit him perfectly. He donned it, left the suite, casually walking down the hall.

There were two white, businessmen-looking guys on the elevator that he boarded, both wearing gray flannel 9 to 5 outfits like the one he had just liberated from the closet he had recently raided. All three rode down silently, George exited the Otis-Built box at the second floor, took the stairs to the garage, fire-wired the first Cadillac that he saw. Gorgeous George drove the car to the east side of town where middle class whites lavished in the sun daily inside of white picket fences. His octoroon skin chameleonically blended in with the boring flannelette projection of these people's conduct. He slid behind the wheel of a maroon Buick 225, pulled slowly off.

When he finally covered all of his tracks, divested himself of the wig, ropes, rig, the light-weight outfit that helped the job succeed, he was $145,590 to the good. The radio was playing low slow music, if listened to you could hear the soulful sound of the Temptations doing "*Just My Imagination*."

George married Taron two months after that pay day. For the sake of his woman he vowed to himself not to do the level ten jobs anymore. He'd do some simple jewelry lifts, some second story sky walks that he had cased that would gross about 45 to 50 thousand a pop. He would do one every two months or so, never falling into a pattern, always altering his M.O. His last project was a cat-walk but it grossed him $89,000.

Chapter 7

Severence

I finally got a chance to meet Severence. Miss talked about him so much that I felt like I knew him slightly, like a fan knows a baseball player. It was odd seeing him. He wore a skirt, a wig, and a mustache. It was a thin pencil-lead piece perched lightly upon his top lip. It threatened to blow away with the wrong wind.

His appearance in The Bubble was as rare as blue diamonds. It was a Wednesday, just about 7:45. I hadn't planned to be in much longer, but, the man that Miss was in love with, the man who had done time, who would kill for the man he loved, was in there and I couldn't pass up the opportunity to check him out from behind the 'Voyeur Glass'.

I dipped into ProLong's office, looked around the entire club then scoped out the individuals. It was like Pro's delivery with the wine. I swirled the room a few times to get a complete taste, then scoped out subtleties. In the ProLong program he checked body weight, aging, finally berry type was his last determination.

When I got to Severence, I could see a murderous, thuggish, tone beneath the surface of manic-schiz. His eyes were screwed back, lava burned the cords of his retina. I could also see a love in him for Miss, subordinate to his effeminate idiosyncrasies. He pulled the chair out for Miss, let him order first, talked softly to him, and made him laugh.

Later I found out that he was a dancer in a powder-puff review. He danced with boa constrictors and pythons to songs like "*Shaft*", "*Let's Stay Together*", and "*Lady Marmalade*".

He did a 10 year bid at San Quentin, that's where he was turned out. I discerned through him that the penitentiary was the final grave yard for hustlers when the game goes sour. It's the result of sport shutting down around the life. When a Pimp can't pimp anymore he'd popped in the pen. When whores get tired and careless they hear the gates slam.

In his days Severence was the Stick-up King. He did about 500 robberies across the country. He was finally shut down when he killed his last mark. That was the first murder of his career (if you can call it a career). The cat he killed was a gangster also. Severence couldn't read that in dude because he was in disguise. What Severence thought was a simple robbery turned into a nasty 187. It was the result of fast reflex and no time to think. It happened so quick that dude was lying there dying where he should have been walking away.

Miss looked at the Voyeur Glass, beckoned me out. That was a first so I didn't know that he was talking to me. He stood up, tossed his wig hair out of his face, put his hand on his hip, and stomped his foot. His over-sized finger pointed to me bidding me over like the girls on 53rd do their tricks. His neck was hopping from side to side, first on his left shoulder then on his right.

I emerged from behind my comfortable security blanket, stepped out into the naked reality of The Bubble more curious than a school of Fool fish. One thing that burned my brain was how did he know that I was looking out of the mirror? Now I was thinking that there was a way that I could be detected so I had to figure out if there was an angle that allowed that or did he just know. I'd figure it out.

"Yes Sweetie, come here! ------ Ain't he adorable! This is the little Man-Doll I been tellin' you 'bout Sevie! --- Little Chicken, this is my husband, Severence!"

I'm sure the term 'love' is relevant now, relevant and elusive. I couldn't see those two together. Their auras were striped and polka dot. I couldn't fit them in the same outfit, but I guess that's grown-folk too!

Now, according to the style of dress they were compatible, they both wore micro mini skirts, wigs, women's jewelry, and women's pumps. Severence had something stuffed under his bra or whatever it was he wore. The something glowed with the shine of breasts but I knew that was impossible. He looked at me and said,

"Hey Sugar-pants! Little Chick! Uh hum! It sure is you! I sat on the steps with you once while Chick was takin' care of some thangs. You was about eight, what is you now, thirteen, fourteen?"

"I'm thirteen."

"You sho' is! An' they never did get that bastard who did that shit huh?"

"Naw."

"But they gone get his ass. He had to be a piece of shit to take out a good ole cat like chick. Sit down chile, so Miss can go back to work. You know my peoples don't you?"

"Who?"

"Egyp, Honey!"

"Egyp? Kevin Bell!?"

"You sound so shocked! Yeah, Kevin is my son."

"But…."

"But nothin'. I wasn't this way forever. I was married, took a fall, the pen broke me honey. They design it to break a man. Especially a young man. You go in strong, an' if you don't die you come out with pieces of you gone, big pieces. Manhood, yeah, most don't admit it, they try to admit an' act like they still hard but it's a lie Baby. Miss tell me you gone be a writer one day?"

"Yeah, I am."

"What you doin' to make that dream real, Chicken?"

"I work on my craft. Sometimes I ask people about themselves. I write their stories after they tell them to me."

"Oooh! Let me tell you a couple. From back in the day, right?"

"Then, now….."

"Okay, okay. Most times I was in a zone. I'd case my mark like a tiger. I could move, baby, all smooth an' quiet, then Bam! I'm all up on whoever. I'm real cool, I'm like, 'This is a robbery, don't make it a murder,' then I'm like, 'Drop your shit in the bag an' don't end up like the last stiff who tried to cross me.' That drama be all in my voice, the air be all still an' pure. I can tell by my mark's eyes how this one gone go. They see the barrel of that long, cold .357 an' they say to they self, 'I wanna live.' So they drop they stuff in my sac, an' I say to 'em take two steps backwards, turn around an' run!"

"Two steps back?"

"Yeah, Honey! I get that from a Mamba, a Voodoo priestess down in New Orleans French Quarters. She say, 'Salute the Lao.' When you lay your money down she say, 'Take two steps back.' When you do, she cover that money with two knifes crossed like a X. Then she throw them bones! I loved her smooth robbery! She give me the word, I say, 'Ooooh!' An' I hit the streets. She say, 'Take with gentle persuasion.'"

"How many people you rob?"

"Shit, chile, five hundred, maybe five fifty."

"Damn! Any violent?"

"Ump, ump, ump! Chick, some of 'em get so close to it that I almost come on my self behind 'em. But most were glossy like silk, ya know? Once, Honey, I get a white boy for $65,000 cash. He steamed! He have the nerve to say he gone get me for that shit. I say you can get me now. I walk slow with your shit for two blocks before I make a dash, but I want your clothes! I holler, Now! His little shriveled dick lookin' all pitiful. I laugh so hard now he really pissed. He call me a black bastard. I laugh some more then leave. He wait for 30 seconds, probably thinkin', then he run out screamin' like some wild animal, 'Aaaaaaahh!' Ha, ha, ha, ha, ha! it's so funny, chile. I turn around an' this naked cracker runnin' at me with both hands straight out like he gone strangle me. I turn, started laughin' some more, shoot a trash can with my magnum. He do a U-turn, he don't break stride, nothin'. Just turn an' keep on runnin' the other way. I see his pink, naked ass hole an' elbows, then he gone!"

"Ha, ha, ha! That's crazy shit!"

"One time I'm casin' this cat, I get on his woman by accident, ole dude he slingin' so I'm gone take him tonight. I watch him break off some keys to some cats in suits, they give him a suitcase full of bread, I see him give it to the girl. She drive off. I'm behind her. I don't want dope, I want the money. I took two keys last night. She drive for 20 minutes, pull up in this place, it's off the road a piece, hid by trees. She stop the car an' light a joint. By this time my car hid in the trees, off some. I'm down low behind some bush. I ease up, in black, hooded an' masked. I pop up like the sun on the side of the horizon, Boom! She scream a little, I say shut the fuck up! I see in her eyes, she not scared, she excited, she know it's a robbery but she excited! She drop the money by my feet, lookin' at my eyes through the mask. Then she pull off her blouse, drop them panties, an' hike up her skirt. I'm lookin' at her fine ass, pussy all up in the air. She say, 'Damn it, you only got 45 minutes before my man gets here."

"I'm holdin' my piece an' stick dick to her an' she scream, 'Hit it! Hit it! Hit it! You Black, thievin' big gun carryin' bastard! Break that Black dick off in me an' leave it up my pussy!' I'm hittin' her an' she scream again,' 'I'm comin' you low-life-big-dick son-of-a-bitch!' I busted that bitch across the head, nutted in her sleepin' ass an' bailed with the dough!"

"Pshhhh! How much?"

"$85,000."

"Damn! Here in town?"

"Naw, that was in Maine, I left there an' came down this way."

"What happened that made you go to the joint?"

"That was a fluke. I see a cat, take him for a Lame. Later I figured he was settin' some other muthafuckas up or somethin'. I peep him openin' a case filled with loot. I wait till he gettin' in a car in a lot, I ooze up an' Bam! 'Drop the bag an' take two steps back.' The bag hit the ground, I look at it an' he pull a .38 out his jacket. Before he could fire it I put one in his heart. I got the cash, made the break an' three weeks later somebody come forward an' say they see the whole thang. They give up license plates and the police tracked me."

"You used your car?"

"Honey, there wasn't no reason not to. I was just chillin' when I peep dude. I jumped into robbery mode but I never figured it would turn into a buck 87. They give me a 15 but let me out with good behavior. Lil' Chick, I'd rather die than go back there. I ain't done nothin' since I been out but dance."

"Dance?"

"Honey, yeah! Check it out, I be on the stage slinkin' like a cat, comin' up all shiny. It's a funky thang! I ease around an' all them mens be callin' my name an' screamin' they words of love to me. I know they can't have me so I drives 'em insane! They left just like the marks I used to take off. They robbed but they think they that (snapped his finger) close. Baby, I'm the one walkin' out with the bread. An' these John's so good to me, I can take, take, take, an' they cry real tears for me to come an' take some more!"

"Damn! What about Egyp?"

"Lawd, he hate that I'm this way, but we right here, (pats his heart). He accepts my choice cause he don't want me to disappear again. He say he rather have a half a ole man than none at all. Oooh ain't he wicked! I don't dress in drag when I go around him, ya dig? Sometime he ask me to take him an' cop him some shoes an' stuff, but he say he can't stand people starin' an' pointin' an' stuff. I can dig that. I respect his wish cause he respect me. Lawd, Chile, when I puts on them bell-bottoms, highboy shirts an' platforms, I'm playin' another role. I'm reinvented! Like when I'm on stage I'm actin' out a role I love! Ooooh, I dig them times, I see him as much as I can, I see him when he wants to see me or he wants somethin'. It's a good mix, you know?"

"Yeah. ------- Where you meet Miss Tur?"

"Can you believe? I'm doin' one of the shoppin' thangs with Egyp an' I see Miss, she with that low-life Dirty Diana. I see that little honey an' I'm crazy inside. My heart flutterin', hands sweatin' ooooh! I'm flushin' now! Any way, Baby is lookin' like somethin' that I would swallow whole! I give Egyp $50 for him to give me 5 minutes alone. He take it an' disappear into the arcade. Miss standin' there lookin' a outfit over, I bump into her shoulder, she turn, I look into her eyes, Hon-ey! I drowned an' ain't come up for air since!"

"So y'all hooked up then?"

"Hell naw! That Diana bitch, she come over cause me an' Miss lookin' into each other's souls, She say, 'What the fuck goin' on?' Miss say, 'it was a accident, he bump me.' Diana say, 'Watch where the fuck you goin',' She take Miss by the hand an' drag her off. Miss look over her shoulder like she sayin', 'Save my life.' I follow 'em out doors an' Diana peep, she run at me like the naked white boy an' I knock her out! I tell Miss I got my son with me but where can I find her later. She say, The Dust Bubble. By the time I get here that night she done dismissed Diana an' I got the prize."

"You in love?"

"Honey, so in love that I do anything for her. This Shady bitch that put his hands on Miss make me want to kill his dog ass twice! Miss say she die I go back to the joint so I chill out. She say if I love her I let it go, it work itself out. It's the hardest thang in the world to do, I NEED to kill Shady."

Chapter 8

Lotta Koochie

There are few things that grown folks do that I totally get. Severence wasn't one of them. They say still waters run deep. This was deeper than the water. My mother showed me in the bible that that thing wasn't cool. But she told me on her own that everybody's got a groove. She said,

"To each what he preach, but if you don't dig it don't knock it."

In here I'm in a rainbow of raggedy righteousness. People view the world with their own misguided concepts and allow madness to nestle into their subconscious and the madness becomes to them reality. Everyone in the club talks to me. They all offer up their concepts of life's reality but I'm thankful that none of them try to put their game in me.

Take Lott, everybody says that she's the premier whore, she can step to a John, turn a corner with him and in less than 7 minutes, come back paid. Once she took a trick off for $137,000 that he had in a briefcase handcuffed to his arm. He was a mob carrier, Lotta was wearing heavy make up and wearing a fall wig when she gave him head. He passed out, she cracked the combination, took the money, filled the case back up with newspapers and left him in the back of his van with no pants or shoes. Dude woke up thinking she had only taken him off for his wallet because the case was still the same weight. He had told her that the case was only filled with financial records from the Mead Corporation.

He took the briefcase in to his boss with a grin on his face. Boss thought that he had taken him off. Shot him right there in the office. The mob boss said that was the second time that the runner had put his hands in the till.

There was never any accusations or recriminating fingers pointed at Koochie. Once she played the head thing on a deputy sheriff in a Texas jail. He passed out, she took the keys and left the state.

Her stories are lined with adventure, mystery, and with retribution. They say inside of her there's a dark, icy wind blowing where her heart used to beat. When Shady hit her with the Heroin and left her in the abandoned building naked, she found Sept and swore to her that she was going to kill him. But she didn't tell anyone else.

That's how she conducted her affairs. She did everything professionally. That's why the day that she and Wee Gee got into the little spat I found it odd. She's known to be as cool and slick as Funn.

A John propositioned her in Vancouver, Washington, gave her $200. They walked off, when they turned down an alley he snatched her by the throat and slapped her. She fell against a wall, he dropped his pants down to his knees. He had his dick in his hand when they found his body. The look of madness covered his face, blood covered his lower extremities, his grip was intense as if holding a prize. Police opened his hand and his severed meat fell limply to the ground.

Because this was just another day, another trick gone crazy, another breeze fanning her face she neglected to mention it to her wife-in –law when she returned to the flat they shared together. The following afternoon the story was on the 12 o'clock news. When her in-law, Boop saw the story flash across the T.V. screen she laughed out loud and said,

"I wonder what the fuck he did to deserve that shit!" Lotta coolly looked at her people and said,

"That faggot muthafucka slapped the holy shit out of me, girl."

Boop's mouth flew open as she stared at Lotta with awe. Lotta laughed and said,

"Honey if you don't shut that a bee will fly right up in there an' make a hive."

September knew what Lotta was capable of. She knew how deep her psychosis ran, she knew a confrontation would result in one person killing, and one person dying. Lotta had seen worse times. Sept knew that it was more pride than anything, this thing with Shady, true, she thought it to be foul and despicable but she knew that Lotta could take her time, plan a strategy and do what she had to do right. Talking her girl down only bought Shady some time. When Lotta did go after dude, it would be calculated, quick, clean. When it happened even if he saw Koochie coming he wouldn't suspect a thing because he would have seen her a hundred other times smiling, laughing, talking stuff.

A dope fiend tried to rob Lotta with a knife, instead of pulling her money out of her bra she pulled a .22 revolver out. Dude dropped his knife, Lotta shot him in the head 3 times and walked away.

The woman is beautiful like a bird of Paradise, she's soft, she's hard, she's poison. There's a side, though, that no one talks about. She's more than diamonds, cleavage, danger. She talks to me when she's not fizzling through lacerated hearts. Before I'd met Lexi she asked me if I had a girlfriend. I told her why I had planned to get with Michelle-Dion for a while. She looked at me for about 45 seconds, like she recognized me from another life time. She said,

"Chicken Bone, choose slowly, baby, an' stay faithful to your choice. Don't try to take a girl an' try to mold her into your fantasy thang. You try to induce change you'll run into trouble, the kind of trouble that you don't ever need, Honey. If you're lookin' for a hotty, don't try to cop plain Jane an' flip her. If you're tryin' to find sweets don't try to pull that out of no hotty. When you choose a girl use your heart. The strongest reason is found in sentiment. If you got real feelin's for Michelle Dion, cop her, be with her. Don't try to pull cause she got pretty lips or a nice ass, listen to your heart, it'll talk to you. It knows things your head will never dream. You hear me?"

"I hear you, Lotta."

"But are you diggin' Auntie?"

"Diggin' you like DAMN!"

"Hush your rotten mouth, Chile! Honey, I gotta get up to get down! I'll catch you down the road. You ate?"

"Just some strawberry short cake."

"What? Muck! Muck Yoo!"

"Hai! Komban wa!"

"Oh Honey, just English! Sweetheart, will you take this boy back there an' hook him up some of your, --you got lamb?"

"Hai!"

"Okay, hook up the Cotes d'Agneau Champvallou. Light on the onion, heavy on the potatoes! An' give him something out of your dessert menu. Put it on my bill."

"Hai! Come."

She loved to call herself my Auntie. Everyone says she's an only child. Miss whispered to me that she eases off from time to time, wears her businesswoman's suits, hair up in a bun, to visit her family. Miss said she had a daughter stashed away somewhere. She keeps that aspect of her life on the down-low because the other side of her life is so scandalous, she'll never involve her family in her wild side. Miss said Lotta's mother raises the little Honey with a few of her other grand children.

Lotta shows up, brings gifts for the whole house, brings money, spends mass quiet time with her daughter teaching her about life, going over her math and English, talking, laughing, and bonding. After a couple of weeks she comes back to her other world. It's hard to say which is her real world. Every yin has a yang. With Lotta, black is black, white is white, there are no grays. I think she needs me. The first time she saw me she came over to me and hugged me, touched my hair, and held my face in both of her hands. I saw something in her eyes that I see in Jamie's eyes at times. Something soft, mild.

"You like lamb?"

"Yeah."

"But you rather have burger an' fry, huh?"

"I'll eat that if the lamb is too hard for you to cook!"

"Ha! Funny Boy! Muck Yoo cook the world domo arigoto gozaimasu!"

"What that mean?"

"An' you sink you know everyting!"

"I don't know Chinese."

"Muck Japanese!"

"Okay, okay! Take a chill pill! Teach me a few words."

"I no speak Chinese!"

"Okay, Japanese, Muck, I'm sorry."

"Hai! You say, sumimasen."

"Soo-me-ma-sin."

"Good, means: Pardon me. Now say ogenki desu ka? It mean 'How are you?"

"Oh-gen-key desu ka?"

"Hai! Now, watakushi wa Chicken desu. Mean, 'My name Chicken'."

"That's busted, wait. Wa-taku-she-wa Chicken Bones desu?"

"Hai! O-mizu wo kudasai, please bring me water."

"Oh-mizu wo….."

"No! You bring water! There!"

"Oh, here you go."

"Arigato! Mean, thanks."

I've been in and out of the kitchen a thousand times, I've see Muck with his pans, herbs, knives, pots, cleaver. But I'd never seen him work like he did that night. After I handed him the water he took a paring knife in his hand and pointed to a stool in the corner and told me to sit there. Once I was seated he started. He took a potato, peeled it so fast, so accurately that the skin unwrapped in one long continuous flow and floated to the table. Two seconds later the potato was chopped then diced with a completely different knife. He pulled the outer skin off of an onion, chopped it in half. With the knife in one hand, a fork in the other, he scooped the onion half up with the knife, flipped it through the air in a tight arc, it landed on the fork. This half he quartered, the other half was diced so fast he looked like he was electrically operated.

He waved the onions and potatoes into his wok, put some lamb chops he had prepared into the oven, pinched a few herbs in the wok, stirred the potato-onion combo. After a few seconds he turned to the potato skin, cut it into two-inch strips. When he took the potato-onion combo out of the wok he drained the peanut oil off, popped that in the oven around the lamb. As soon as he closed the door to the oven he spun and tossed the skins into the steaming peanut oil. He was moving around the kitchen like a ballet dancer and the room filled up with the most exotically exciting aromas that blended together like a conducted symphony. I sat and watched his hands and feet move in choreographed harmony like those of a ballerina.

He stayed busy until the meal was lavishly spread out on my black octagon plates. There was lamb chops, stir-fry broccoli with snow peas, potato and onions, macaroon soufflé. The arrangement was so elaborate that I didn't want to eat it, just looking at it was fulfilling. The meal was a work of art. Objects d'art. I sat looking at it so long that Muck came at me with his famous cleaver. He said.

"You no eat? I cook you! Stir fry chicken Bone!"

"Hold it Muck! It just looks so good I don't want to touch it. I ain't never seen nothing so beautiful in my life."

"Thank you. Muck cook for palate an' eye. Chicken eat Muck's labor of love."

"My man!"

"No, Chicken Bone my man! You good kid, why you hang out in gin joint?"

"Just a job. Why you hang out here?"

"Mr. ProLong, he save wife life. Some very bad men try to rob and kill, he no like what he see, step up, kill two of them."

"Here in town?"

"No, San Francisco near Pacific Ocean. He walking away, I say to wife, 'You know we owe life to him.' Wife bleeding but we know he get away so I go after. Wife no hurt bad though. Muck fall on knees, beg Mister ProLong, 'Please allow Muck to repay you.' I tell boss, 'Confucius say, if man save life you owe man life of service."

"Confucius? Ain't he Chinese?"

"Yeah, but talk good huh?"

"Yep!"

"Boss say, 'Can you cook?' I say I study culinary arts in France. He say you want to repay? I give you job. He take wife to hospital, later fly wife, children, an' Muck all out here. Now everyting fine! Wife fine, two children love it here. Not all the shooting like in San Francisco."

"Dang, ProLong's that thang!"

"Good man. Very good. Pay Muck too much!"

"Me too!"

"Muck no put Cote d'Agneau on Miss Lotta Bill. Tomorrow Muck cook you seafood gumbo, Ann Tea recipe. Your mother know you hang in gin joint?"

"Yeah."

"She no trip?"

"Ha, ha, ha! Naw she don't, well, yeah, she did at first but she knows that I'm just a trash-errand boy."

"You more than that."

"Huh?"

"Mr. ProLong, he love you like son. He tell everyone, 'You no corrupt him, no drugs, no guns, noting!'' He say he hear somebody tell you how to hustle streets they have big-big trouble from him. Confucius say, 'Advise them to the best of ability an' guide them properly. Only stop when there is no hope for success."

"An' he's guidin' me good an' proper!"

"Muck know. --- He say you get good grade in school go to college, huh?"

"I'm tryin' to get a scholarship."

"He say you good enough, but if they no give he send you to any school in world."

"Damn! I ain't never heard about that!"

"You still no heard. You say Muck Yoo spill his guts, you get to be on menu next to big mouth bass!"

"You crazy, Muck! How old are your children?"

"13 an' 16, girl 16 name Ashita, boy name Akick."

"Ashita Yoo and Akick Yoo?"

"Hai!"

"Muck, you off the hook! Why you like to cook?"

"Muck like to excite! Confucius say, 'Ensure that those who are near are pleased an' those who are far are attracted.' Muck bring them from far an' please when they arrive!"

"You think ProLong'll send me to college if they don't give me a scholarship!"

"Damn right!" I looked at him like he was nuts. He said: "I hear Miss say that all times! Mr. ProLong say he love you, say he wish so bad you was real son, but since you not it no matter. He take you under his arm."

"Under his wing?"

"Hey! You no like how Muck Yoo talk?"

"Yeah, yeah! Put the cleaver down! Did Pro tell every body that stuff?"

"No, he tell everybody no corrupt. He tell Muck Yoo everyting else. He say, 'Muck you keep eye on boy, you see him fall in lions pit you tell.'"

"Lions pit…? Okay! Okay!"

"So Muck like Diadokoro Kioto!"

"What's that?"

"Kitchen Guardian Angel."

I finished eating and got started on my work. People would start showing up for the dinner hour soon. I was blasted by the revelation that Pro was looking over my shoulder, a man of his wisdom and stature was an asset to anyone. It was a pleasure just to know him, let alone have him say he loves me. That's when I realized why everyone in the place kept me out of their game. And for that I was eternally grateful. Momma told me that praying lips weren't as holy as helping hands. I didn't know what she meant at the time but it was clear from that point on. I had never really dwelt on the thought that nobody kicked game of the streets because they gave me real love, that's where my mind was housed.

I was proud of Pro's affection for me. I didn't have any idea why he would get into me so deep. But I did note how he spent a lot of time with me talking and discussing my future plans. He was a light house, he steered me forever towards the shore home.

There were times that my curiosity took me to the door steps of game. He'd just tell me that I really didn't want to know the answers to the questions that I had asked. He said he'd teach me about life, women, and how to run an honest business but he'd never help me get filled up with street.

I told him my questions were merely inquisitiveness not the impulse or desire to walk that walk. His answer to that was if we have an hour to rap, we'll rap about Dow Jones and admission scores, not what a cat can say to a chick to make her turn a trick for him. I really had no desire for that style of life it was just one of those enigmas that my mind tried to unravel while I sat around. I'd look at September, beautiful, robust, gentle. I'd wonder why she had turned to the profession of degradation. I mean I've seen Glory, Mousie, Kookie, Kandi, and 30 or 40 other women who contributed to the numbers of the avocation. Most of them, probably because I don't know them personally, I can see hooking. But Sept, Lotta, Dee Lux, some of the main ones, I couldn't understand for the life of me what was the fascination, what was said that made the Earth-Goddess do the most uncool of things.

And even though they are or were hookers, the oddity was, my mind never coupled these women to the business. The talks I have with them radiate with a son-mother air. They all have fresh out-looks, they all are wise beyond the paint and posh. I see emotion in the eyes that thousands have gazed into but very, very few have had the pleasure of experiencing.

Chapter 9

Dee Lux

"Hey Little Chick! Come an' give me a hug an' a Kiss Sweetie!"

"Hey Dee!"

"You are growin' up kid! Agin' years in days. Nice little outfit an' do! Who did your hair?"

"Willie."

"Over at Wanda's Weave an' Dax Wax?"

"Yep."

"Oh yeah. I shoulda known. He's the bomb. I had so many weaves hooked up at Wanda's. Shit, I think I paid for that El Dog that her man Willie sportin'!"

"That's a fine El!"

"Shoot, that ain't nothin', you'll have a brand new one as soon as you graduate from high school."

"Right! I can't buy one of them."

"Hush Boy! Stick out yur tongue."

"Huh?"

"You heard me! ----- Yeah! Uh hum! I'm gone tell you now, no woman will ever have the pleasure of feelin' the heat from that thang if you spill a word of what I said."

"But you ain't said nothin'."

"Come here. ---- Pro gone get you one. But don't you ever tell nobody. An' don't get to buddyin' up to him cause you know, cause boy, he'll know somebody done spilled an' he'll trace that drip back to me. Damn it, he know I can't keep no secrets, I don't know why the hell he tell me shit. Chick shit be burnin' up inside of my ass! I hear it I gotta say it to some body else! Don't ever rob no bank an' tell me! The word'll be out 'fore the 6 o'clock news! An' I know I'm dead wrong!"

It seems to me that everything that Pro wanted to tell me he would tell someone else and they would rush it to me with speed of fire. It's like he'd sneak into my heart through the back door and just be there when I looked up.

Being hip to the nature of all the folks he talked to, he knew they would leak, I would hear everything that he said and I would swell up with it. I guessed he didn't like to be lavished with 'Thank you, Thank yous'. Or maybe he didn't want me to think he was giving me charity. I don't know, some more grown folk concepts that further puzzle me. I only knew for sure that I had Momma on one side, ProLong on the other side and I wanted to make both of them proud of me. I didn't need to construct change in my life I was doing good, my thing was to be consistent with it. That meant keeping my head on straight. What's so hard about that?

"Hey Baby Boy!"

"B-Down! What's up cat? You holler at Momma?"

"Yeah, she on regular time today. She would have been home before you came here but she had to run out to the hospital...."

"Hospital? What's up?!!"

"Chill B. Her job requires that she have an annual check up."

"Oh, it's that time again? MAN! You had me gone!"

"You awright. I gotta get to work, a little dinner music, ya know!"

"Yeah, play that Al Green "Let's Stay Together'."

"Bet that. ---- Good evenin' Bubble Dusters, I'm the man with the plan, the man on the scene, the man who has an' plays most everything. Tonight for your personal, specific pleasure I'd like to start my

Segue show with 5 in a row. This first piece goes out to everybody's number one son, Little Chicken. The groove off of my stack of wax is Al Green's "Let's Stay Together." Come on up an' make a request. You like it, you say it, you say it, I'll play it."

That Al Green piece just grew on me. I was all the way into party music like, "Brick House", "Kung Fu Fighting", "Freak Out", and "Lady Marmalade". Then Lexi had me listening to the slow grooves like Al Green so much that we started calling it 'Our Song'. She told me "Just My Imagination" was how she thought about me before we hooked up.

She's so deep that she told me I take the darkness out of nights and bring sunshine to her when it's raining. Come to think of it I not only had Momma and ProLong in my corner but I had Lex and all the people who adopted me as their son, nephew, and brother holding up ends for me. I talked to Momma about most of them, when I called Monkey Paw by his street name she said, "Tommy Paine! He's so sweet." She put real names to most of the people I talked about from the Bubble. For her not to be in the life she knew more or as much about the streets as I did.

Two days ago Ann Tea told me she heard that Shady tried to break into Pro's Money Green 'Lack. She said Pro peeped him because he had left his Cubans in the ride and went back to get them. He caught Shady messing with the handle on the driver's side and blasted at him with his .22 derringer. I saw a look on his face when he came back from getting his cigars. I knew something had irked him but he wouldn't rap to me about it. He told Muck about the break in, Muck told Ann Tea, Ann told me and probably a hundred other people.

I saw Sept and Fancie right after but I don't think they knew because they would have been kicking it about it, instead they were tripping off of some girl who came up from Danville Illinois or some place.

"Fancie, who is this Chile?"

"Girl, this is Josette..."

"Hi, hi, hi! An' you're…?"

"September….."

"September, September, September, no, can't say I have…"

"Have what Girlfriend?"

"Met a September, No, I've met an April, May, June, a Helen March. Never a September, that's an unusual tag, who's idea was it?"

"The nurse at the hospital wrote my name on the wrong line. I was born on September 14th, she has September Flower born on Valencia 14th."

"That explains it perfectly. You think I'll work out?"

"Work out what Honey?"

"Oh, Fancie, you didn't ask her?"

"Ask me what Fan?"

"Girl, she just wants to sing. I just told her you was the leader of the Hearts."

"Yeah! Heart Attacks! That sings, sings like a Marvin Gaye song….!"

"So you tryin' to get into the Hearts?"

"Oh, no, no, no! I know the Heart Attacks! Every thing you do is three part harmony. Three part. Three part absolutely! No, no, no! Fancie, tell her! Tell her!"

"She's not tryin' to get into the Heart Attacks."

"Oh, September, September, September! Doesn't that just scream Fancie! No, no, no, September, I could just say that all day…..!"

"No! Stop! Get to the point!"

"Yes, yes, the point. I'd like to open for you. I think that the Hearts are such a major influence on the genre of three part harmony. You, Ana Stasia, an' Pretty Penni, Oh! Pretty Penni, Pretty Penni, Pretty Penni!"

"Fancie!"

"Sept, come on! Listen to her….."

"Later, sing a song for me later. I got a head ache right now. I gotta …"

Fancie pushes Josette.

"Loving' you
Is more than just a dream come true
An' every time that we oooh!
I'm more in love with you
La la la la la, la la la la la
La la la la la la la la la
Do do do do do oooh, ooh ooh ooh ooh ooh ooh!"

"Damn girl! My head ache's gone. I ain't heard no shit like that since I was in church! Hell yeah! I'm callin' the girls to the back chile, they gotta hear your ass! Ana Stasia be writin' some cold ass shit, I know she'll want you to do some of her pieces! Come on! Fan! Girl, shit!"

Josette had my mouth and eyes wide with the Minnie Riperton song. It sounded exactly like the Diva! The octaves were exact and the woman Josette was too easy to look at! At first I thought she was too dingy to sing, just another wanna be. Sept probably had the same concept. Some things just can't be explained away. Sept took Josette into the room where she and the girls dress.

Between records, while B. Down was spinning, quiet rap I could hear the girls either singing or giggling and talking fast. I loved it, they had an atmosphere when they were together. Sept was tight with Lotta and Pretti was aces with Fancie but they almost never took them past the red door. They'd sit with their cats at the round table just to the left of the bar while Miss served them flaming drinks and complementary reflections out of this mental reservoir.

Even when Lotta and Sept were doing their thing they ran to the restroom not to the red room. I knew what was up because they would come out wiping at their noses.

When I saw Dew Rag flicking and pulling at his nose I asked ProLong was it because the powder made their noses tingle or what.

Pro told me that the dope that made people's noses run where they had to wipe all the time was cut with a milk sugar called dextrose.

He said it was a cheap product and the users had to put up with this diminutive side effect, among others. He said emaciation was another side effect that extreme users had to deal with. However there were extremes like Boosting Betty, Fat Frank, Too Raw Paul, who abused the white powder but hadn't lost a single pound. He said that some people who snorted or shot coke loss weight because the hydrochloride, the base, caused appetite loss. I told him that somebody must have taken the hydrochloride out of Fat Freddy's coke because I saw him pulling at his nose while eating Chateau Briand, macaroni and cheese, sweet potatoes with tiny peas, 2 baked potatoes, Muck Yoo salad with French dressing and croutons. He also had Tropical ginger bread, wine soufflé, peach meringue, and coconut cream pie, with diet coke.

He told me to get out of the office and get to work. When I closed the door, I heard him laughing loud and long. I was sure that tears were running down his face. I found out some small thing about him at that moment, he would laugh with me, tell jokes, listen to them, but if anything took him out of composure, even for a second, he wouldn't allow it to show in front of anyone. So I went on with my work, laughing with him, but alone.

Chapter 10

September

The next night I came to work Ana Stasia and Pretty were there. It was unusual to see them so early. Ever since the first day me and Arch met them I noticed they all came in just around 11 o'clock. But that night they were there early and with them there was something thick in the air, like the cicatrix down the side of Dead Fo' Real's cheek. Something dense, nasty, disturbing.

The usual vivaciousness that hung easily in the stratus was replaced with a grim resonance. Even Miss's usual effeminate façade was dropped. He wore of course the wig, the make up, the micro mini, but his face was hard tonight, his voice heavy like rusted lead.

There had to be something indecorous going down if Miss abdicated his feminine cover, displayed his doggish acrimonious side. When Shady slapped him, called him out of his name, he did little more than swoon and accept it.

I decided I wouldn't wait for them to include me in the conversation. I knew they would hold off as long as possible because it looked and felt like some grown folk undertakings. I knew they would skip over me like a flat rock on a river if I didn't butt in.

I wasn't in the mood for a subterfuge not when it was of the caliber that caused the whole of The Bubble to freeze up, I'd been a part of this place for 9 months and everything that went down I was talked to about. Yet when I walked in a strained hush fell over the room, voices dropped, nothing was up on the other side of the room but the lights. The need to remain aloof was out weighed by the desire to know. I went over. I looked into everyone's face, they all sat straight up but dropped their heads down. I said,

"Miss, what's goin' on?"

The room then filled with a slow deafening silence, his face hardened, his chest swelled with slow, deep breaths.

"Somebody…"

"Somebody your ass…"

"Okay Ana! Honey, obviously Shady tried to rape Sept. He beat her down so bad that we lost her for a few minutes. But some cat who worked at St. Andrews Hospital was comin' by an' saw it. He shot his gun in the air an' Shady took off."

"Dude went to check on Sept an' she wasn't breathin'. He did the whole mouth-to mouth thang an' brought her back. After that he started hollerin' an' somebody called the ambulance."

"The son-of-a-bitch stabbed her 4 times. She got a whole lot of cuts on her hands an' arms which means she fought him back. She got multiple contusions, black eyes, an' swollen lips. We're waitin' to see ProLong so we can all go over to the hospital. We've been callin' but can't get a hold of him. You know what he be doin' most of the time, where you think he at?"

A sick feeling covered me like a long afternoon shadow. To think that he said we lost her for a few minutes. Lost her? She died? We lost her?

"What you think Chick?" Tears burned as I spoke,

"He at the hospital."

"Damn! I didn't think of that. Chick, she gone be awright. Look, I'm drivin'. Tell Muck we all goin' over to the hospital, if he not there at least he'll know where we at."

"Awright. Don't leave me, I'm ridin' with y'all."

"We know."

The ride over was as quiet as moon beams. After Miss ran down all of the injury statistics there wasn't much to talk about. Everyone was either praying for Sept's recovery and regular brain and motor functions or praying for the death of Shady. Ana and Pretty loved Sept like she was their actual heart. It was Sept who found Ana and brought her to Funn. Ana was sleeping in an abandoned building. Funn took her in, cleaned her up and gave her a job. He had her dropping off bundles to his workers while he rode behind and collected cash. It wasn't until Sept heard her singing "Midnight Train To Georgia" that she came up with the idea to form the Heart Attacks.

At the time Sept was with Funn and Pretty was with ProLong. The two of them had worked some spots together. While standing around in the rain of boredom they would blend their melodious voices together then laugh at the end of each song.

The Heart Attacks still laugh big at the end of songs they're practicing. Now there

were two Heart Attacks in the ride, silent, sad, forlorn. September was their Heart, they were her Attacks. If she didn't come through these two girls wouldn't be the same. Sept gave them their attitude. She's the reason they got out of the flat-back game, out of the dark alleys and into the spot lights.

When the trio first started singing they did sets on Fridays, and Saturdays, but their popularity, sexy moves, fresh grooves made the people scream for them every night. Sept made sure they gave the people sexy but not raunchy. She took the Hearts across the country 8 times, into the studio 4 times.

"Nurse?"

"Yes, may I help you?"

"Yes, we're lookin' for 'September Flower."

"Oh yes, I know that name. She's in 4721-B. She's out of danger, all vitals have stabilized. If it hadn't been for the E.M.T. driver on the scene the doctors say she would have been lost forever."

"You mean she would have just died there in the filthy street?"

"I Think so, the first few moments are critical if the heart stops. If the heart doesn't get blood and oxygen to the brain within 9 minutes the patient will have permanent brain damage. I'm told that only seconds after her heart stopped the E.M.T. driver brought her back. Doctors say they think there'll be complete recovery."

"Thank God! How long?"

"We just have to let the body heal. Is she a fighter?"

"Oh yeah!"

"Then, there you go!"

"Can we see her?"

"I'm gone let y'all in for about 5 minutes, awright?"

"Five minutes is cool! Thanks!"

Our hearts beat as one person's as we walked down the hall. We turned the corner and found her room on the left. We walked in quietly, eased up to the bed, and looked down on what looked like death.

"Can she hear us?"

"I'm hurt, not deaf!"

"Sept!"

"Sept!"

"Girl!"

"Tember!"

"Ooh! Little Chicken, you came too? My Little Love Bone! You still in love with me?"

"Yeah!"

"Even lookin' like this?"

"If God took my sight, I'd still see your beauty. None of this matters."

"You're so special! Ana, Pretty, Miss, thanks for comin' to check up on me. I love y'all! What's up with that hoe-all Shady?"

"Girl…."

"I'm gone kill that bitch. I've had enough of his ass. He killed the only man that ever treated me special….. Oh God!" Her hand flew to her mouth.

"Sept you told me Big…."

"Chicken come back! Stop him Miss!"

"Lawd!"

Miss caught me half way to the elevator. I don't know where I was going. It was too far to be trying to run home but I felt like I needed to run. Just run until I dropped. My eyes were clouded, blazing drops of liquid salt were cutting tracks in my cheeks and staining my shirt. Miss caught me and held me in his arms like a big brother would and let me cry. The fire tears burned through to my Soul in those seconds. Miss put his hands on my shoulders, stepped back, looked into my eyes. He said,

"Chicken Bone, this ain't about you, or me, or Big Chicken, right now our girl is in there, she died Chick, now she's back, we're her rock. You gotta bear your troubles with the patience of an acorn waitin' to be an oak. You gotta walk back in there, with nothin' on your mind except your love for that woman, if you don't it'll tear her down like ghetto projects Chile. You understand me?"

"Yeah."

"Good, now buoy yourself. Sept feels bad about springin' this on you, but if you don't show her you forgive her an' love her, she might lament to death. You wanna kill that Honey?"

"Never."

"I don't think you do either. Wipe your face. Take some deep breaths. --- Good Baby. Ready? Ready?"

"Yeah I'm ready, Marvin!"

"Oh, hell naw! No you didn't go there!"

"Ha, ha, ha!"

"You rat! Lead the way."

I held my head up high and walked back down the hall back to Sept's room. I felt bad because Chicken was killed by a slouch, I felt bad for the sake of feeling bad. But I was here for Sept, not me.

"Oh Chicken Little, I'm so sorry….."

"No Valencia, I'm sorry, Sweetheart. I'm gone be here for you everyday. You tell me what you want, or what you need, you tired of this hospital food you tell me that an' I'll have Muck fix you the finest food that he can cook."

"Valencia, huh? You do still love me!"

"Tember, I'll love you until the wings fly off!"

"Then kiss these blistered lips."

"For real?"

"Real, Baby! ----- Ooooh! No tongue boy!"

"Girl, I didn't …"

Everybody broke out laughing and talking, and everything at the same time. Talking about everything except Shady, and rape and death. The nurse came after a while to corral us out. We kissed Sept, and on the way out of the room she said,

"Y'all do me a favor?" We all concurred.

"While I'm here an' y'all come to see me, please don't nobody talk about Shady to me, huh?"

"Not a word Sweets."

"Not a word."

I walked over to her and took her soft, caramel hand into mine, kissed it and said,

"Not a word, not a thought till you walk out."

"I love you Little Chicken. My Big Man!"

"I love you too Tember."

"Boyfriend, get outta here 'fore I break down like a jilted bride!"

"Bye!"

"Bye!"

At least on the way out we were back to talking and laughing again. As if we had made the request ourselves, none of us talked about Shady, or pain or our lacerated Heart. Because we were talking so much we took a wrong turn. We ended up in the lounge facing ProLong.

"Pro!"

"Hi Honey!"

"No wonder the joint is closed down, all the help is here."

"Oooh! It's all my fault…."

"Chill out. Y'all go back, have Muck fix y'all something. Tell him to burn me a Cornish hen in milk an' celery. I want Rum Bumble with the whipped cream sprinkled with toasted almonds. I'm goin' to see Baby now. Chick, I'm glad you came. You're her heart. She thinks she birthed you. Now y'all get on outta here before I have to hire a new crew."

"See ya!"

"Chicken Bone, you said he was out here. I was wonderin' all the time we was in there where he was, he been here all the time."

"An' he knows she's awright ."

"How you know?"

"Cause he read us."

"For real! He's the coldest! He can look in your eyes an' tell what you seen yesterday."

"I should call Muck an' have him to put me somethin' on."

"Shoot! Let's all eat Lobster…"

"Thermadore!!!"

"Cool! We don't have to call for that, Miss, just get us back safe!"

"Shut up Chile. I was all in a hurry tryin' to get us here. Fish, I had to see my Baby! She'll be fine. I thought cause she was gone for a second that she would be all fucked up or somethin'. Shit a little make up an' a trip to Wanda's Weave House an' she in there!"

"Ooooh! No you ain't talkin' 'bout her wig Miss Fish!"

"Ana, you jive turkey, don't you try to bend all outta shape! I'm droppin' you off on the way!"

"Speakin' of wigs! Miss Thang!"

"No you didn't! No you didn't Fish! Honey your wig an' your make up need hollerin' at!"

"Pull over Miss Thang! You talk that talk, now walk that walk!"

"Mm mmm! Still waters do run deep! I ain't even messin' with you in your granny dress! Don't all them clothes make you feel like a blimp Chile!?"

"Hell naw! Cause under them I know I'm a naked woman!"

"Ooooooh! Ho no, no, no, no, no, no! Girl I will slap the waves out your weave!"

"With them big ass Man hands, I guess so!"

"Lawd Jesus! Save my life! Take me now! Take me 'fore this Fish fry me in the front seat!"

We were laughing so hard by the time we got to The Bubble that we almost forgot we had just been to the hospital.

I'd never seen Sept so vulnerable. But even lying there in that bed she was like Chicken said, tall, proud, strong.

It was business as usual at The Bubble, the restrooms, the kitchen, the bar, the lounge,

the tables. It seemed so empty though, knowing that Sept wouldn't be there at all that night. I went on and did some of my work while Muck cooked for us. By the time we finished eating, (Miss inhaled his lobster). ProLong came in. He said the nurse sanctioned him 15 minutes after he slipped her $50.

He pulled me to the side and personally gave me his word that Sept would be alright in no time. He said she had been hinting about taking a Jamaican cruise for months, said when she healed he would take her. I smiled and told him to take care of her, she would heal quicker if she knew he was behind her. I went around, hollered at everybody, left.

I just wanted to get home and talk to Lex. It had been a long 2 ½ hours. My mind was tired, my body, weary. I donned my Chuck Taylors and Levis then left.

The night was motionless, empty. This act of Shady's was an encroachment on our tranquil environment. Inside of The Bubble we were exempt from the putridity of the rest of the world. The walls offered us a haven. Even the din was euphonious and calming. Any small disturbance of that peace was quickly and quietly syncopated by the colossus Monkey Paw. Plus the presence of McRotten and his pernicious bodyguard Sixkill, covered the crowd like an umbrage which caused most of the patrons to keep themselves in check.

People came to The Bubble not for trouble but for the sheer lavishness of the atmosphere. They came to be good to themselves. They all knew once they passed through the doors that if they weren't good to themselves it was no one to blame but themselves. So they came, exuberant, munificent, disabusing themselves of any penny-pinching concepts. Of course in life there was duplicity, procrastination, prototypical conspicuous consumption, allegorical smiles on the faces of cons and cabalistic but inside we were family. Most of us, inside, were quiescent, tranquil, all of us, however, were home.

Chapter 11

Apartment in Paradise

September's stay in the hospital was brief, she of course had to return a couple of times for surgery, skin graphs, follow ups. The doctor said that she mainly needed a lot of rest. He checked her X-rays and found no hairline fractures or anomalies. He told her if she were to start feeling any sort of dizziness that she was to return immediately to his office.

Pro moved some of her essential items into his apartment so he could keep a close watch on her. He had a nurse on call that lived in the building and a girl in the penthouse who waited on Sept hand and foot. She told me later it was like an apartment in paradise.

Pro paid for extensive grafting that covered the cuts so well that one would have to be staring or using a microscope to even see where they were. Sept went under the blade 4 times before all of the scars were veiled. Because of our support her inner wounds healed as quickly as those which she sustained by the hands of the low life.

There was a woman who cooked for Sept who specialized in back woods Soul Food. She was a 250 pound, jolly, pot and pan rattling, big laughing, mother figurine. Who treated Sept like she was her daughter. She told Sept that Pro didn't have to pay her for cooking, she said she loved cooking so well that she could stay in the kitchen 24 hours.

Sept had manicures, hair styles, pedicures, and two women that she suspected of being lovers who fitted her for the most beautiful dresses and gowns. Every outfit they made came with a hat and some came with gloves. Then there was the man who called himself LeSole' who came with over 100 styles of shoes. Pro told her to get at least one of each.

The only thing that he didn't supply her with was white powder but she wasn't a chronic user anyway. She only snorted with her girl Lotta from time to time. There was, however, plenty of Dom Perignon and Remy Martin on hand if she just wanted to buzz.

The Hearts came by at least once a day and they all sung, drank and laughed. Sept thought that Pro was about to propose at least 4 times while she was there. He had the ability to make the air rare and tranquil while he talked to her. Even though he didn't propose the excitement of anticipation was bigger than any rush she had had in the last ten years.

Chapter 12

School

I half slept that night like something alien was in the room with me. Not a terminating alien, this one was more or less an ALF-type presence. I kind of wanted to sit up and hear my ALF spit some whimsical jive but I knew I had an English exam the next day so I at least tried to sleep. I lay half wanting to sit up, half knowing I needed rest.

The silent sedation of sleep was stronger than the small pest in the back of my mind. As I lay still in the watery stream of false sleep I thought of Lexi and Sept. Thought is it's own reward. I was able to imagine Lexi at Sept's age. I thought and saw what Lexi would look like after we graduated and went to college. Her hair was still long and flowing, her eyes, soft and trusting, seeing me, scooping me, following me across the room, sizing me up.

Her mouth, scrupulous, playful, now passive and reserved, spilled resonant, melodious laughter that filled me beyond the brim. A touch from her hand and we sat upon a star, which floated above clouds, which floated above seas. She turned to face me and her lips easily brushed mine, then my alarm went off and woke me up. I sat straight up in the bed to see the first light of morning stealing in through the cracks of my blinds.

I wanted to talk to Lexi, so I hurried with the washing and the dressing. I felt good. Alive. I thought about how lucky I was to have Lexi now and not later in life when things were so complicated, so grown up. Everything that we did was so unadorned and moderate compared to the grown world. Nothing in grown world read like Sunday comics. Even their wakeups must be majestic. There would be no need for me to later say, "I wish I knew then what I know now." I know now. Their lives are totally complex, and a lot of the complications are orbited by two monstrosities; sex, and money. As children we didn't have a concept of either. As teenagers we became painfully aware of both. We start to jostle and scratch for them until we get all discombobulated, but by the time we reach adulthood we're C. then A. then U.G.H.T. in the deluge.

Tralla told me during first period that Lexi wasn't coming to school today. She said that if I got lonely that I could find her some place on the school ground and she would take Lexi's place. Pshhhh! Lex is going to see it one day and clean out her car, but until then she'll be rolling with the Tralla.

The English exam was a slam dunk, I linked some verbs, dangled some participles, turned some passive verbs into active ones and gave two examples of chiasmus' for extra credit.

In math we did some long division, converted some fractions to decimals. Nothing real big. Class dragged on with out Lex, yet I calmly endured. There was always those few people who were just now hearing about the car wash and were excited and wanted to work for me. They were always animated so that put a little something-something in the hours away from my Pooh. I took a few numbers, promised to call as soon as I needed some help. I thought that perhaps I should expand.

Me and Arch kicked it most of the day. He and Kevin ended up telling me about letters that they got from Duh-Duh. He was locked up in Juvie for pulling a knife on a clerk at A&P Grocery Store, then breaking out the front window. He's been there almost 9 months. He got locked up not long after I met Sept. No one had heard anything from him until Arch and Kev got the letters. He told Arch that he wrote me and for me to write him back as soon as I get his scribe.

When I arrived home the mail was in the box, the first thing I saw was the envelope with Duh-Duh's real name on it. I'd known him for the last 6 years and had only heard his name 4 or 5 times. The letter said,

Inmate mail – Mervin Canton,

2130 W. Broad Street,

Columbus, Ohio 43223

T.I.C.O. Balson Cottage

I wondered what he wrote like. I mean diction. His hand writing was very neat, neater than most cats and fancier than some female's scripts. The letter was eloquently expressed, it was hard to realize that Duh-Duh was so intelligent. The letter read:

What's up Bones? *Feb. 9, 1977*

There's no reason for me to ask you how you are or what you been up to. Shit man, I know you're handling yourself. You're the only one of our friends that I know won't end up in here.

My mother wrote me once man, and asked me what it was like in here. I wrote at the top of the page "Worse". I said "Momma, it's worse than anything you could imagine. There are some young kids who have to do time until they're 21 and most of them have thrown in the towel."

Chicken, man, some of these young dudes let a cat turn them out because they're threatened with violence or owe a couple of packs out.

Man, I listen to the news about the Viet Nam War, all of the death, destruction, and disease are nothing compared to the loss of freedom.

There's a question, 'What's the difference between death row and a life sentence?' The answer is; nothing. Death row, though offers a quicker demise, is less tormenting, while doing a life sentence you die a thousand times. The latter is the slow agonizing death

but they both end up in the same agonizing scenario. You lament then expire. Nothing's the same Chick. None of the eggs in the middle of the night stuff. Or what about the warm midnight snack thing? It doesn't apply here. No cereal and milk after lockdown kid. No girls, Chick, none. Even the concept of freedom of speech is non applicable here. The C/O's can talk as crazy as they want to but if you bite, you're ass-out. There are women working here. You can spend time in solitary for what they call 'Reckless eyeballing.' Or worse Chick, establishing a relationship. Think of you, out there, on a large cruise ship sailing along, stopping at junction meeting people, having pleasurable times, making memories. Now, think of me as being on a raft, in turbulent waters, feeding off of the garbage that floats to the top. With me there are no pleasant moments, the memories are not my own, I got stories from a thousand different cats in my head blending with my own making

me question even what I think.

Man, I'd rather be with tramps and thieves than to be here one more minute. Yesterday the Disciples blessed my Bunkie in. Can you believe that? He's in here locked into this system then he loses his mind and gets locked into another system. They have some'blood up, blood down' rule that they go by. That means they make you bleed when they bless you in and they spill your blood if you try to get out.

I've died a little bit everyday since I've been here. I went into a shell because I refused to eccept this shit here as normal. I stayed folded up like a love letter in an old shoe box. The sun didn't even shine on me. Now bro, I've come out of the shell and decided to reach out. I realized what you offer. I hollered at Kevin and Archibald, you know? I did that because we're all cool, but I want to come home and have some positive people in my corner, you dig? Some body that I can rap with that won't bring up the words 'rip off or mack'.

I have a screening review in 4 months and the unit manager says because of my record here I have a hell of a chance of coming home then. Write me back as soon as you catch a minute. By the way, how's Yogi? I miss everything about life now, even somebody else's girl.

Stay away from the traps, man, it ain't nothing nice in here.

Be up! Stay up!

Your Cat, Duh-Duh

P.S. How are the Hearts? Man!

I never really thought about the joint much. I've heard stories from cats like Severence, and Knock Out, The Bully, but none of the stories have ever moved me to emotion before. At first I was standing by the window reading, some how along the line my subconscious moved me over to the edge of the bed where I sat riveted even after the P.S.

It's evident that Mervin understood what he'd driven himself to and subsequently he will rectify the wrong and get back on line. I stood up after a few long, hard minutes of thinking, walked to the window and looked out. Nothing was trivial that I drank in with my eyes. Not the ball in front of the steps, the kid with the news paper riding by with his bike, the robin singing over by my mother's daisies. Every color, every movement of the leaves held grand implications to my eyes.

Nothing, not even the tangibles, was consistent with the state of being yesterday. Even human order made me realize that it was disorder. In this life I know I have hope, desire, motion. In the existence that Duh wrote about those things that I've taken for granted are luxuries, luxuries that even the strongest inmates can't muscle.

I decided I'd write him later tonight when I'd have plenty of time to think of what I wanted to say to him.

I had my white Chuck Taylors on today. The skies had been radiant all afternoon, even now they were lovely and clear. My walk to work was different, I was stopped by a kid who asked me where he could get a stick of weed. I told him to go home and talk it over with his mother and if she told him where to go then he could cop. If she didn't then he should give up the idea. He looked at me like I had just broken out of a cage then he bailed.

I reached The Bubble about 5:00. Pro was in a meeting with McRotten so I just pulled out my rags and polish and went to work. By the time I looked up it was 7:15 so I packed my rags. I stepped outside, looked around and oozed into the night. Like the smell of shit that comes in on a sudden breeze I heard the high pitched voice of Darren Jerr.

"Hey Low life, get over here."

He came up so suddenly that it startled me and my heart beat could be heard through my chest.

"You're officer, Dick, an' you're Barren something right?"

"You smart ass bastard."

A quick wit was all I could think of to calm my heart. I knew these guys like to show their teeth, but they don't bite. Since I'd seen them last I hadn't even tried to figure out when I'd see them again.

"I'm tired of savin' your Goddamn ass, punk. First, you know who the fuck we are, it's Dix not dick. Second, another one of your wise cracks an' I'll take your ass down an' lock you the fuck up."

"Ass hole, we're gonna ask you a few questions an' you're gonna answer them or get your head split. Got it?" I looked at them both with a stoic calm but inside I was laughing so hard that it would have been totally offensive if a single 'ha' had broken through my relaxed façade.

"Okay, little faggot, everybody's heard about the murder that occurred last night."

"Murder......?"

"Playin' innocent won't help you, we know you know everything that goes down in that little shit hole there."

"That's right you little son-of-a-bitch, now what we want to know is what you done heard about the killin'!"

“I don’t even have the slightest idea of what you’re talkin’ about,”

“We’re talkin’ about the murder of Walter Head.”

“Walter Head?”

“Shady Goddamn it! Tell us who killed Shady last night no more than 3 blocks from here.”

“I just got in the club a couple of hours ago. No one was in there who would have talked to me. I don’t know anything, I haven’t heard anything.”

“I’m gonna tell you a secret little bitch. I don’t like you, you got your little smug ass attitude, you hang around with scum buckets, an’ think you’re better than honest workin’ people.”

“I’m just an honest workin’ trash man….”

“Bitch!” His hand went back.

“Dix! Not here! Listen boy, I know you try to help Jamie out from time to time, you get good grades in school an’ you wanna do the right thing. That’s why I stop him some times. You wanna do the right thing don’t you?”

“Yeah.”

“Yeah see. Okay, we’re gonna give you 2 days to find out what’s up.

“Somebody in there’s gonna tell you who did it then you’ll tell me. I’ll take care of them an’ you’ll keep helpin’ your momma.”

“But nigga, if you don’t come up with somethin’, hell, we’ll pin this shit on you an’ have you tied up on a murder rap. You know what they do to little pretty boys like you in the joint!?”

“No, but I’m sure you do, an’ you’ll tell me huh?”

“Bastard!”

That time he did get one swing off that landed in my stomach, it folded me and the sudden impact dropped me to the ground, hard.

“Hey! You no-good son-of-a-bitch! Get the fuck off of him!”

Never had the sound of Pretty’s voice been sweeter. She rushed past the dinky duo and helped me up. There was strength in those small hands of hers.

“You awright Baby.?”

"Yeah, I'm cool."

"You bastards will be hearin' from McRotten so fuckin' soon your heads will swim. Now you pea-brained, Barney an' Fred, donut-dunkin', flat-shoe, cock suckers can get in your funky ass, beat-down cruiser an' bail or you can stand here an' deal with Mc right now!"

She had pushed the buzzer and now the door was opening.

"We'll talk to both of you bitches. An' you remember what we said boy, you got two days."

They rushed to the car, hit the ignition and sped off. Prolong was coming out of Mc's office and rushed over.

"What's up! What happened?"

"I came up an' Chick was on the ground. Dix an' Jerr were over him."

"They put their hands on you?"

"Dix hit me but it's cool."

"No it ain't. Take him home Pretty, you drivin'?"

"Yeah, my ride's right out side."

"Good. It'll be taken care of. I don't want either of you to EVER mention this to anyone. Do you both understand?"

"Yeah."

"I understand."

"Chick, they won't ever bother you again. So what's this all about?"

"They was drillin' me about a murder that happened last night. They say they want me to find out who did it an' tell them."

"Find out?"

"Yeah, they want me to talk to e'rybody here an' snitch on the killer."

"Man, fuck them. They're the pigs, not you." It was odd to hear him curse.

"They say if I don't tell them what happened in two days they'll charge me with the murder an' have me tied up in court."

"They've over stepped their bounds." He was totally calm again.

"Pretty, where's the rest of the girls?"

"They should be on the way."

"Good, I rung you all over half hour ago. Chick, you need anything?"

"Naw, I ate an' e'rything else is smooth."

"Cool. I'll see you tomorrow. You need me, call me, huh?"

Me and Pretty pulled out. She was cool like not a lot had happened. She pulled me over to her side of the seat, put her arm around me as she drove. I was sitting there feeling her heat. She had a very light perfume on that I probably wouldn't have noted if she hadn't pulled me so close to her.

I felt a swelling in my loins that I hadn't ever felt where Pretty was concerned. Her arm around me, to her, was merely a security blanket. To me it was a log on a fire that had never been lit. She looked at me where we were a few blocks from my house then asked me,

"You gone be okay an' able to keep this to yourself?"

"Yeah, I'm not really hurt, the punch just caught me off guard."

"Those hoes! Look, you need to holler at somebody you find me or Pro, cool?"

"I'm cool." When she put the car in park I said, "Can I have a hug?"

"Boy, I see your stuff tryin' to bust through your jeans! You wouldn't be tryin' to cop a cheap feel off your Auntie, now would you?"

"Ooooh!"

"Ooooh your butt! Here….(Hugged me) Now, take your little nasty self in there. Lord knows what sort of sordid business you gone be up to in there all by yourself! You better call your girl!"

"That's messed up!"

"Get out! Give me a kiss first. Hey! No tongue! I'm tellin' Pro!"

"I ain't give you no tongue!"

"Better not!"

"God, you crazy!"

There is a hand that reaches down and touches us all! Some people aren't even woke long enough to verify it. They're either absorbed in their hard drive to bring down bread, or so busy chasing the sexual satisfaction train that they scarcely notice subtleties.

I never would have believed that I would one day get wood from a grown woman. This particular woman was around me so much, calling me her nephew that I started to believe I was. When her arm pulled me next to her I looked up at her ruby lips, inhaled her scent and that moment became pivotal. I thought of Duh's words, "No girls, Chick, None!" I had a girl and was wrapped up in the arms of a beautiful woman right in front of my house.

I was touched by all of the subtleties, that the people of The Bubble chose me to love and not some other kid, that I'm out here and not in there with Duh-Duh, that I had a mother who cared and loved me more than she loved herself, that I had a girlfriend who adored me and loved me with a passion uncontested. Nothing was too small to thank the Lord for right now. And so I laud him.

Chapter 13

Lexi

"Hello?"

"Hi."

"Tom-Tom! Hi Baby!"

"How you feel?"

"I feel different."

"Why?"

"I'm in love."

"I'm in love with you too Baby."

"I got a letter from Duh-Duh, he's still locked up. He said some stuff."

"What?"

"It's just a real heavy letter, about bein' locked away from e'rything you love. How he turned off to the world until it almost broke him."

"That's sad."

"I know. To lose those you love is a hurtin' thang. It made me think about you."

"You can't lose me. You thinkin' 'bout getting' locked down or somethin'?"

"Naw. But I don't think he planned to get messed up either."

"But Tom-Tom you're so much different than Duh-Duh, Kevin,

Archie, Rick, most of the boys you hang with. I can see it in their eyes, they're wild as rodeos. But you, you got sense, you got direction, you got me. I'm in your corner, if I see you goin' left, I'll talk you out of it. I'll talk till my throat falls off..."

"Until your throat falls off?"

"You know what I mean Goofy! I'll help you. Me an' your mother, we'll put e'rything back in pocket. You don't even have to worry about the Duh-Duh situation, he's got a good heart, he took a wrong turn but I don't think that's a sign of what he'll be doin' for the rest of his life. He just didn't have nobody lookin' over his shoulder tellin' him that they love him. Does my love matter to you?"

"Because you're mine, I don't even want to die an' go to Heaven. I could live on Earth, or dwell in Hell forever if you're by my side. Can I see you now?"

"Boy!"

"Just for a minute."

"You better hurry up! I'll be on the porch on the swing. What time is it?"

"About 8:15."

"Cool, you know I can stay out till 9, so get on over here! An' bring me them kisses."

It didn't take me more than ten minutes to get to Lexi's house. But on the way over I thought to myself that I was really running from the letter I had to write Duh. I was stuck, thinking how even the inconsistencies of living were constant. Just below the surface they waited to manifest. But my worse day wasn't as bad as a second in Duh-Duh's life. I decided not to obsess. Instead I'd picture myself in Lexi's arms even before I turned her corner.

"Hey!"

"Shhh!"

"Come here!"

"Mmmmmmm!"

"Don't try to drown yourself in my water girl! I really needed to see you, hold you, look in your eyes. It's been into three days."

"Tom-Tom, you look so serious."

"Don't trip on me, I'm goin' through a light weight thang, but seein' you set me on my feet again. That crazy Tralla, she the one told me you wasn't gone be at school, leave it to Tra to be the bearer of the worse news. But you awright huh?"

"Yeah. Just crampin'. Tralla's just like your boys! I don't know what's gone happen to her down the line. She might end up like that man they found the other night."

"What man?"

"Oh, they found some man in a Chevy Impala not far from where you work. He was shot in the head 4 times point blank."

"Damn, what they sayin'?"

"They sayin' he was a dope addict an' they think his death was drug related. The police say they ain't got no clues. They just say he was shot with a .22."

"Did they find the gun?"

"Naw, they say the man must have known the person who shot him cause when he died he was eatin' some Church's Chicken, he had a mouth full an' had a breast in his hand."

"Like this?"

"Pshh!! I don't think Church's Chicken got this much meat on their breasts!!"

"You insatiable thang!"

"You better shut up an' kiss me some more before my mother an' sister come an' get me!"

Lex, my rejuvenation. I could easily write Duh now. I think I just needed to get back to my teenage world after that punch in the stomach.

At work the next day I heard they arrested Dew Rag on a robbery charge an' found a .22 revolver on him. He was being held on suspicion of murder pending a ballistic report. The robbery victim came in and picked someone else out of the line up, he was cleared of robbery and held for murder. Out of the rain, into the river.

Later Sept told me that the police picked Lotta up in the area of the murder. Fat ass Dix said he knows that she carries a .22 from time to time. Sept had to track Long Greene down so he could go make her bail. She wasn't packing heat at the time of her arrest.

At first Long was extremely pissed because at the time he was on the track collecting paper from his girls. He was pissed because he knew this break in the action could cost him a chunk. He'd have to pay the fine, bail, and if not back on the track quick enough one or two of his workers might peel back the top and cop from Cowboy, he was seen on the track with that China-white horse and the white-girl.

Most of Greene's girls shot dope, but Lotta snorted hers because she hated needles. One of her friends caught hepatitis from a dirty outfit. Greene chilled out when he got downtown because the bail was considerably lower than anticipated. Lotta was only charged with disorderly conduct and resisting. He snatched her out, dropped her off and got on with his business of pimping.

Everything was normal at The Bubble, but I still had a strange grinding feeling in my stomach that gave me a slight vibration. There was really some grown folks stuff going on, whatever it was it was strong enough to make Dix and Darren Jerr continue to hassle people coming out of the club even after being forewarned by Sixkill. I knew that I would see them again.

I didn't want to take another punch in the stomach. It wasn't so much the pain as it was these two low-life sack's of shit had the nerve to put their hands on me and they were dirtier than muddy Mississippi water. Even though there wasn't a lot I could do, there was a lot that I wanted to do. I carried no mixed emotions where they were concerned. They had the nerve to say they would charge me with this murder if I didn't help them do the job they're paid for, then to top it off they went as far as to mention Jamie. If I had my way.

I didn't have the slightest idea how long a murder investigation went on especially one involving a dope addict. Usually in a case like this the police say,

"He's a junky. Fuck him!" Got what he deserved." But ProLong said these two fools were trying to get Brownie points and were taking up the investigating on their own.

"Miss?"

"What Honey?"

"What'll happen if they catch the person who killed Shady? You think they'll pass the death sentence?"

"I don't even know Baby. I'm just glad they ain't picked up Sevie for it. She had told a few peoples that she NEEDED to kill Shady! Chile! I told her ass not to be shootin' her mouth off like that. What I'm gone do Chick? If the word get out she been sayin' that? An' Lawd knows she do carry a .22. Oh Gawd! What if she really did do it? Chick! Chick! Baby, I die if it was really Sevie! Oh, Lawd, Gawd!"

"Miss! Miss! You workin' yourself into a frenzy. You fillin' your head with unpleasant representations that have no basis. Most apprehensions are excited by the unknown an' it causes a mildew to grow on all pleasures. Talk to Severence, ask him if he did it, if not, don't trip. They arrested Lotta on the same false charges, but she's home, or out or wherever she is. But any way Miss, if he did say it they still need collateral proof to support their claims."

"Damn Chicken!------ I remember that day you first went down them stairs with me. Chile, inside you was shakin' like drug store crap! To think you was in a dark, dank, hole with a boy-lovin' freak. Naw Honey, don't deny your fears, I wouldda been a bit shaky too! But that's not what I'm talkin' about. Chile, you done grown up! Miss used to give you all the good advice, now you givin' me the straight dope! Baby, we gone be awright. Sit, you got ProLong as your mentor an' I got you. Lawd! You done sent a Dream in here an' he gone point out the way to sanity for Miss! I'm gone do like you say, I'm gone ask my Baby, an' she say no, I quit worrin'!"

I was glad he felt consoled, but I still had a dark cloud hanging over head. These two fools had woodies for me. I knew that Mc would reprimand them for hasseling anyone coming out of the club which means he'll get on them and they would lean on me harder. If I hadn't spent so much time behind the Voyeur Glass I wouldn't be thinking about any of this so much. Where they were concerned I was experiencing a multiplicity of dark emotions. I wanted to eradicate them but I was just a kid. I knew that what ever I had to do involved a lot of ducking and dodging. Neither of those scum drops were the type who took threats lightly. They were dangerous, two Black cops in a precinct full of White Irishmen who told Nigger jokes. To be accepted they shuffled and laughed with their subordinates. To further prove they were a part of the crew they put their feet on the necks of as many Black folds as they could during and after their shift was over.

They used to live around here but were so zealous that they tried to bust all of the H. dealers on their days off and after hours. One Thursday, at exactly 5:15, 15 minutes after they clocked in, both of their houses blew up. Since neither were married no one was hurt. The warning only served as a catalyst which launched a hate attack on what they called Nigger trash.

They swept through the hoe-stroll and snatched up about a dozen women, busted in on most of the after-hours joints, popped numbers runners, and a numerous amount of pimps. Most of the busts were shaky and about 90% of the people in their sweep got out on technicalities.

They pulled up on ProLong and McRotten at the same time. Mc was ready to wet them both but Pro told him that was more trouble than it was worth. They discussed it later and decided to put them on the pay roll. Pro's words to Mc were,

"Keep your friends near, your enemies nearer."

The police were paid once a month to stay out of the hustlers' way and not to hassle the customers. One of the main criterion was that they never set foot in the club. McRotten sent his muscle, Sixkill to deliver the payment each month. Six liked to catch them in awkward and compromising positions when he brought the payment. He's pulled up on them when they were pissing or dumping or freaking with hookers they had busted. Every time he crashed in on them Mc logged it in a book. He kept an accurate account of their movements.

Chapter 14

Back To The Bubble

When Sept was released from the hospital Pro threw an 'Out and About' party for her. Josette sung three of the pieces that Ana wrote for her. Afterwards "The Attacks" were called to the stage. They did three of the songs that Sept was featured in. Ana Stasia and Pretty Penni were the only ones on stage, as a joke they sung only the background and their solos. In spots where September was supposed to sing a spotlight hit her mike and there was silence.

Everyone laughed so hard that it seemed like we were at a Richard Pryor concert. Finally Miss broke down and cried. He admitted that he had loved September from the time he first saw her and she would be the only woman in the world that he would convert for. He raised the roof with that revelation!

A few weeks ago while I was working, Pretty came in. I had on some music and was doing Michael Jackson's patented moves. At the party Pretty called me up to the stage and made me dance for Sept. She whispered and said that if I didn't dance she would tell everybody that I tried to slip her some tongue when she dropped me off. I told her I'd get her butt for trying to blackmail me with a lie.

B. Down introduced me, "Ladies an' Gents an' Miss!! The Dust Bubble proudly presents the hardest workin' "Get-me-this-get-me-that"

Man in the business! Little Chicken Bone dancin' to Kool an' The Gang's "*Hollywood Swingin'.*"

I got up there with my shirt and tie and Stacy Adams and went to work. When I moon walked everybody howled. I felt electricity shoot through me like Haley's Comet. During the last 20 or 30 seconds of the record Miss got on stage and tried to do Mike's moves. I laughed so hard that my stomach hurt for ten minutes.

Muck made Seafood gumbo, Ann Tea made Choux pastry ring with chocolate sauce served with rose petal ice cream. We ate, they drank, everybody partied. There is nothing like festive activities to take your mind off of pain or problems. When my time started running out Pretty volunteered to take me home.

"Come on Sweets, say good night."

"See y'all later. Sept, I love you. Glad you're out an' about!"

"See ya' Little Chicken." She kissed my mouth.

Just as we thought, the dregs of public service were hovering like flies over shit. They saw me with Pretty, turned their spotlight on, then turned it off again. She pulled of slowly but hey didn't follow. They were trying to bread into me but Pro had already schooled me on how to deal with them.

Even if I did know anything they couldn't force me to tell what I knew so there was really no need for me to panic.

"Penni, where you meet Pro?"

"Baby Doll, um um! I was in Hackensack, New Jersey workin' tables, breakin' my back tryin' to get enough to pay rent, groceries, an' get a cute little dress out of the lay-by. I was so far behind that the dust of them in front of me had settled an' fell back to the ground. I had this cat I dug, sho dug drugs more than he did me. He kicked my ass, took my check, I got thrown out an' moved in with this girl Peach. She fell in love with me. Lord Chick, she did some things to me that I ain't thought no woman ever could do. But her love was worse than Ernie's. She was so obsessed that she wouldn't let me work. She gave me pocket money an' stuff, an' bought me everything that I wanted though. One day, she see me askin' the stock boy at the store for a price, she beat me down in the store. Beat him too. Police took her, found out she was wanted for a felony somewhere. I stayed in the house till I couldn't take it no more. One day I got dressed, went for a walk, an' this long, black El Dorado come pullin' up next to me. This fine man gets out an' says, 'Baby, I been lookin' for you all day.' I say, 'How you lookin' for me an' you don't know me?' He say, 'Girl, I've known you forever. Recently you been hurt by love, physically an' emotionally. I know that's over an' will never happen again.'"

"How you sure?" I say.

"Cause once you get in the front seat of this El, nobody in their right mind would ever put their hands on you again, Especially me." I believed him too.

"But I don't know you!" I tell him.

"But you know people, look in my eyes, tell me if you see a person who would ever harm you in there."

"Chick, I looked in them eyes for an hour, you know? I saw some kind of magic there. I saw the man who I dreamed about. One who knew things, had been places. I say, "Can we go back to my place an' pick up my suitcase?" He said,

"You don't need it unless it's full of cash."

"Ain't no cash in it."

"Shit, you really don't need it then."

"What about my clothes?"

"Oh, didn't I say we're goin' shoppin soon as we cross the state line?"

"To where! New York?"

"New York, then Chi Town, Miami, Amarillo, Vegas..."

"Vegas? Oh lord! You gone take me to Vegas? Wait—wait—What's your name?"

"ProLong."

"Hi ProLong, My name's Penni."

"Pretty Penni. Let's ride."

"I couldn't believe it, Baby! That was 12 years ago. Chick he ain't never lied. He told me we was gone make money, buy houses, an' cars. An' he promised me I would only work for 5 years then retire for the life. 5 years form the day we met he put this ring on my finger an' handed me a bank book in my name. He's a bad muthafucka baby. ----- No need in me askin' you where you met him. He thinks you're his, did you know that?"

"Muck told me."

"I knew he would. Muck's so damn sensitive! Pro saved his wife."

"He told me that too."

"I was there. He's so cool normally, non-violent, you know? These cats tried to kill Muck an' his wife. They beat Muck down, had a gun to his head, one dude stabbed ole girl once she went down. Pro pulled up, walked over there, shot the cat wit the gun in the throat, shot the other cat in the head, turned around a' was comin' back to the car. Muck had ran to his wife then to Pro. He begged Pro to let him repay him, Pro moved them out here. He gave them an apartment in one of his buildings an' Muck ended up buyin' one of Pro's houses."

"Pshhh! He's like some kind of hero!"

"He's more than that baby. I could tell you some things about my Gracious Gangster, but you gotta go. Where's my hug? An' don't let them hands roam. I know you wanna do me baby, but you gotta get over them feelin's!"

"Damn, you're worse than Terrible!"

"But you love you some Penni! How's Lex?"

"She's fine."

"Chick, you be good to her. Give her respect. Be true to your word. If things work out gravy, you marry her. You got the qualities of a true man, don't you ever break down to the streets. Now Pro, he's a different type of man. He's a hustler with a heart. They say there's one of them in every million out there. But Baby, I know for a fact That he regrets that he didn't finish high school an' go to college, in spite of all that he has. He's gone make sure you do though. You hear me?"

"Too near ya, not to hear ya!"

"I'm tellin' you, I'll kick your ass myself if you fuck up. You love me?"

"More than I love cooked food!"

"You love ProLong?"

"Without a doubt."

"Then you promise me now."

"I promise that I'll stay in school, got to college, an not slip you the tongue!"

"I love you rat-ass. Tell Jamie I'll holler at her one day."

"You mean my Momma?"

"How many Jamie's you know?"

"Damn!"

"Don't make me soap your mouth! Now get out!"

"Bye Beautiful."

I had so many people down with me there was no reason for me to fail. But how many escorts would it take to shake the tiny-brain-Two out of my tree? Chick told me that life was full of the reoccurrence of disappointments, these two offered me an explanation to what I didn't understand then. We're born of the parents but it's the teacher that makes us the man, I have a hundred teachers who I attribute my journey to manhood to.

I remember when I was in the third grade, I told the teacher about Razz the Bully, he had been on my back for a while and it was tiring. She took him out, scolded him, and he rode my back until the fifth grade when his family moved. It was always the same, "You ratted me out!" Through Razz I knew the characters of Dix and Darren Jerr. They're bullies that burn with an unrighteous indignation that's driving me towards madness.

I guess at their moves from time to time even though I know that speculation is a dangerous pastime. The thing about that is ProLong taught me to anticipate my opponent's moves, but for the time being I'll close the chapter on negative connotation and get ready to do some serious letter writing.

That night the house was still. A carefree breeze danced through an open dining room window enhancing my thoughts of Lexi. They emerged delicate, inviting. Her beauty whispered to me loudest during the soft, noiseless hours of evening. They showed me that everything with meaning is in something intangible, love, desire, trust, hope, the untouchables. I opted to fill my letter with these, or at least some of these.

Duh-Duh, What's up Cat?   Feb. 14, 1977
I take it by the context of your letter that you've done some big-big rationalization since you've been there, good. Duh, I ain't never trying to preach but since we're cats I feel like I can speak out. You're intelligent and ain't nothing wrong with your mind. You need to take the little time you're there and keep your face buried in some books. Don't get bent by cats who say "Geek", "Bookworm", "Nerd". Those are devices used by all of them cats who are too lazy to try to push themselves. They think the game they're picking up will get them over all of the humps of life but that game will only get them slammed back in there.
Remember what Malcolm said, "If you want to hide something from a Black Man, write it down." Don't be one of the ones that written knowledge is hidden from.
I understand t a degree what you mean by the word "Worse", I have a close friend out here who spent time locked down. He did 10. He's given me some in depth concepts of what goes on in there. He made me see a clear picture. Just like you he say that I should avoid the traps that jam you in that den of inequity. As for the question Duh, there is a difference between death row and life sentence. The difference is life. As long as you're alive Duh, you got a chance. You say you die a million times doing a life sentence man, that means you

live a million times. Accentuate the positive Bro.

I feel your rap about the eggs, The snack, the cereal and milk, and especially the girls. But dig man, all of those things that we take for granted out here you've formed a tight appreciation for. Something not so dark has emerged out of that.

As far as your life raft scenario, Duh-Duh, you're not alone. I'm down for you, you write me, call me once a week, what ever you need or need me to do you let me know. At least the rest of the time you're there you can be comfortable.

And don't tell me you don't have memories, you got plenty of them. Shit man, the thing at the Circle was off the hook. We partied all the way there and back! And don't think I didn't peep you coppin' a feel on Sheila! Man! I saw that look on her face Duh, she was diggin' you like Oh Yeah! Come on out and step up, if she's with someone, don't sweat it, cop you another one.

For every day that you think you've died in there, we'll get together and live twice as large out here, Cool?

Oh, Yogi's cool. Still gorgeous as hell! She's not with anybody right now, you ought to write her too! Shit, the way you scribe, you can knock her ass. She digs that flowery shit! It'll surprise her to read your letters, Man, shit you surprised me! You ought to write some poetry.

You remember Alexis? We've been together for a while. I'm in love man! Hell yeah, I said it! We're like book ends. She's the Yin, I'm the Yang! Can you feel me? We sprung each other though!

Come on out man. We got people to see, things to do, places to be! I'm still running the car wash! I'm gone hook you up. Oh, the Hearts are cool! September was in the hospital for a while but she's out and as beautiful as a Love story man.

Ana Stasia's still writing some bomb ass songs. Pretty Penni dropped me off at home tonight! Them's my peeps! All of them. I think they going back to the studio soon. They found another girl

named Josette, she opens for them, she's cold! Sounds like Minnie Ripperton. You gotta hear her! You ain't gone believe it.
I'm gone try to get you in The Bubble for a second one of these Sundays. The place is super-plush.
I'm going to send you some pictures of me and Lexi and some of the other Honey's in the neighborhood.
You got the number, call as soon as you get the letter. I usually be at home between 3 and 5, then I'm back about (most of the time) just around 9:30. So if you don't catch me keep calling. I pay the phone bill so Momma won't even trip, Cool?
I miss you man, Be up! Stay up!
Chicken Bones

Once I signed the letter I had a good look on my face. I know I gave Duh a little something to look forward to. I'm going to try to hook him up with a job besides the car wash. But the car wash will be cool for a start. I'll probably cut him $2.00 a ride so he can make about $40.00 a day there.

ProLong has some property, maybe he can clean out some apartments that people have moved out of or something. We'll figure it out. I got all of these people helping me, I can give back by helping someone else. Let that first someone be the Duh-duh.

I stared up at the stars for a while, tried to see the man in the moon. I went to bed after a piece of Jamie's Apple Crumble (ala mode of course).

Chapter 15

Chillin'

Being at school, for me, is like being on a vacation the first half of the day. I don't trip off of any of the kids though. I don't think I'm better than any of them, I'm the same it's just that going to school after being in The Bubble the night before is like coming home from Mardi Gras and attending your brother's 6th year birthday party. You endure, but you're not in to it. Most days I can't wait to clock into work.

The other day I got to work about 5 till 5 and Ana Stasia met me at the door. Which was an oddity.

"Hey Chick! Come here! Come here!"

"Ana, what's up?"

"Boy, Sit! Sit! Sit!"

"What?"

"Okay, them muthafuckas was called to the east side of town, you know, the Write Project?"

"Where all them White motor cycle dudes live at?"

"Yeah! Well they got called over, they say it was a lead to the Shady murder. They was over there an' a few of them cats pulled up an' they started hasselin' them an' ended takin' no less than 15 bullets each!"

"Who we talkin' about?"

"Fat ass Dix an' Darren Jerr!"

"Damn!"

"I'm sayin! See? They go around fuckin' with people an' somebody feed they ass to the worms!"

"So they both dead?"

"Hell yeah! 15 each! Police had Write Town penned down. 'Bout a hunnit police was there. They couldn't come up with no evidence, no lead, no clue, no nothin'! They say all them White folks was sayin' they ain't even hear no gun shots. Some dude was takin' out his trash an' found them. They was dead 5 ½ hours before the police was even called."

"Man," my Mother said, "What goes around comes back."

"I knew you wanted to hear that!"

"You ain't never lied."

The rest of the night I had a luster like I was wearing silk and walking in the sun. I had been obsessing over this Dix-Darren-thing, then the candle by which they had been reading the bones they threw suddenly snuffed. Fate! Man!

Chapter 16

Shady

Big Chick told me that life has a resolve of its own, events sometimes unfold both interesting and extraordinarily. The tawdry and sordid characters that were a part of the night life were impossible for me to avoid. They were as much a part of the life as the stars were a part of the night. The cold and callous were subtly mixed with the crowd of people who I had come to know and love. The whole scene was a blend of good and ugly, a tart-sweet type of work.

Dix and Darrenger! Pshhh! Dick and Jerk! They eased up on me like slinking cats, pounced on my body and tried to lean on my emotions. They struck at some nerves. No more. Then Shady. What's in a name? Well, Walter, his name is his story, his life, his way. There were a hundred reasons, 99 of them legit for people wanting him dead. He was one of the worse people that I had ever encountered. He has raped, robbed, cheated and killed.

There were hundreds of people coming and going during the course of a week at The Bubble. Never before him had I touched shoulders with a cat who everybody hated. If it wasn't one thing, Shady had his hand up another. There were hustlers, cons, macks, thieves, tramps, and flatbacks. Most of them seem to have a street that they refuse to cross. I say this because not all of them have earned the title of

"Straight Sleaze."

The Shady cat was the Sultan of Sleaze. To him nothing had significance, worth. I heard about how he robbed his mother and father. Tied them up in the basement and nobody found them for 48 hours 48 minutes. This time they spent in total darkness.

He slept with his sister, that started when she was 12, he was 16. That lasted until she was 20 when she got married and left town with her new groom.

He robbed dope houses, killed runners and dealers. The police couldn't hold him. He'd been at it so long that he learned how to slip the system.

He beat up Mrs. Jones, gave her a heart attack. She recovered but it seemed like he beat the sense out of her. After she returned from the hospital she started talking to herself and screaming at airplanes. They say he took 78 dollars and 54 cents from her and left her on the side walk for dead.

Another person he beat up was an old man. He left him so bloody in the street that dogs started ripping and tearing at his flesh. They ate his face completely off by the time the police came. Cops had to shoot the dogs to get to the body.

He slapped Miss, raped Lotta, tried to cross Funn and ProLong. He broke into Stone Love's house then burned it down to the ground to cover his sloppy tracks. Stone found out, killed Shady's brother and the sultan didn't even come to the funeral.

When September came home and sat me down, she was so full of emotion that it brought me to unembarrassed tears. She drew close, in spite of the uncool look in her eyes, I easily inhaled the Chanel Perfume that she wore. My eyes went to her hair, dancing across her perfect light-chocolate complexion. Even though I had Lexi, I still dug Sept in a way that I know would never come together. I had a bona fide crush on her. To be at work some days was an inspiring event instead of a salt mine. She was too smart not to know I was froze on her.

I looked into her eyes and her lips parted, her perfect teeth brought cadence to her glossy butterflies. I knew that something wasn't quite right with me because I started to find delight in whatever it was I was reading on her face. Then her words came, low, under soft sobs that escaped from her soul, escaped in spurts. I lost her eyes beneath the now flowing tears.

"Shady killed my girl Dee Lux. He tried to rape her and take Funn's cash. This was the second time he assaulted her. She wasn't takin' it no more, so she pulled her knife. He hit her with a lamp an' stabbed her with her own knife 37 times. I'm tired of him killin' all of my friends. It was him at the accident ----- with your father. He was driving, pulled Eric under the wheel, got out an' ran. He got wind two years later that Chicken bones was lookin' for him for killin' Kwan, an' he killed Chick. Right on 5th Street. Chick didn't even know nothin' about the rumor. The bastard put a gun to my head an' made me fuck. I thought he was gone kill me every second his funky ass was in me. I kept prayin', Lord, please don't let him kill me. I swear I'll do some good if you let me live. So I'm tellin' you so you can tell your Mother an' she can have the case reopened. I'll testify."

"That son-of-a-bitch! -------- I need time to think if I want to stir up all of that in my Mother. Give me a couple of days. I'll see if she wants to go to court. ---- I gotta go."

"Okay Sweetheart, I'm gonna go in there an' tell ProLong you're thinkin' of tellin' Jamie."

"I'll see you Sept."

I walked over to her, put my arms around her, drew her close. That was the first time I had embraced the object of my profound affection without a thought of perversity. That was the first time that I didn't think of her as a piece of Girl candy. I loved her for reasons without names.

I walked out, used my spare key to open ProLong's passenger door. I hit the button in the glove compartment and the trunk popped open. I closed the glove box, then the door, ran around to the back of the car, got the .22 out. I took it home and pulled out some of the rubber gloves that I'd brought back with me from work. I removed the bullets, wiped the gun down while wearing the gloves to remove all prints, mine and Pro's. I eased out of the back door and down the alley.

A few days in a row I had seen Shady parked over by the junk yard. I walked without thought, without fear. When I stepped to his car he was sitting there eating chicken with a bottle of Rose sitting next to him. When he looked over I was standing there with the heat in my hand. I looked him in the eyes when he looked my way. He said,

"You little bastard, I know who the fuck you are. Give me that god damn gun!"

He reached up and I shot him. It was easier than I thought. The first bullet went through his left eye. I put the gun up to his head and pulled the trigger three more times. I put the last two slugs in his heart.

I ran through the Euclid alley down to the end, took a left that led me to the river. It seemed like I was running on air. But I wasn't running with fear. I selectively chose pieces of this un-Eden of pain and duplicity. I sought the diversions in shadows. I was cognizant that everyone in this life no matter how diminutive a role they played, is as capable as the worse of society's dregs.

I was like the cat hanging with the perfume salesman, I smelled like the thugs and the murderers that I'd come to grow fond of. However there was no regret in my course of action. I saw my movements more as classical than course, more distinguished than crude.

I knew the river like I knew The Bubble, I'd spent many of my playful hours there. I took the gun to the deepest part. Removed the spent shells, flung them in. I put the gun down on a slab of concrete, smashed it with a large smooth boulder. I threw all of the pieces into the moonlit water one by one. I filled my gloves with rocks, cast them far out over the whispering river. I watched the cool water cover them as the moon beams covered it. The soft ripples were all that was left of the rapid splashes that I had just made. The splashes that no one heard but me.

I walked back up the steps, spilled out, blended into the night.

I woke up the next day, went to school and contrary to rumor concerning these sorts of affairs, I had no remorse. I took a math test, finished in good time, took the extra credit test, got another A+.

When Jamie arrived home from work I had prepared for her Muck Yoo's Chicken Tetrazzini, Leek and potato soup, and a Caesar Salad. I'd been Muck-Dancing in the kitchen since I'd gotten home, but I was glad to be there. I didn't know when or if I was going to tell Jamie, but I had rectified the things that had torn her gentle heart to unusable ribbons. That was two weeks ago.

I came out of the bedroom last Saturday and Sept was in the living room talking with Jamie. Momma was crying, a relieved cry. She told Sept, "Thanks for tellin' me girl! I'll talk to Tommy about it, ---- I love the chain an' charm you sent me." She looked up and saw me then said,

"There's our baby now!"

"Hey Chicken!"

"Hi Sept!"

"Remember what I told you about school! You know I love you Kid! Jamie, me an' the girls are gonna sing at his graduation!"

"I love you too Tember!"

"Girl, I'll see you. Call me sometimes!"

"I will!"

"Bye Baby!"

"See ya!"

When she left Momma sat me down real quiet and calm. She said,

"Baby, September told me how some police had harassed you a couple of times. She said those same cops met with misfortune. They was called over to the east end and ended up getting' killed. The guy Shady, Walter Head, who got killed a while ago was the one who killed Kwan an' Chicken Bone."

"What?!"

"Yeah Baby! The Lord done answered my prayin'! They got him Sweetheart. They don't know who. They say there was no witnesses, no weapon, no clues. Nobody knows who did it. They say that Dix an' Darren Jerr were close to the answer an' whoever it was must have been the ones who killed them. Now the investigation is on the shelf until the gun shows up!"

"Momma, this is the first time you been excited in a good while! Look at you glowin'! I'm glad to see you lookin' so pretty!"

"Thanks Honey! Now that's behind us you can get on with your schoolin', an' we can get on with our business of life."

Monday ProLong drove his red El Dorado to the school. When I stepped to the car the passenger side window smoothly hid itself in its safe, comfortable, red haven.

He didn't say a word, he just held his hand out, diamond down, palm up. I reached up to my neck, took my chain off so I could remove his key. I handed it to him. He captured my hand with his, covered it with the other hand that had until now been resting peacefully on the steering wheel.

He looked into my eyes and a smile played at the corners of his mouth, at the corners of his eyes. This was the same smile that I'd gotten used to seeing when we played the voyeur Game, but only when I'd gotten the characters right.

No words were spoken, he tossed the key into the ash tray, I stepped two steps back, the window rolled up, the Lack pulled off. I saw the right turn signal, then I lost sight of the Cadillac El Dorado behind the corner of the school.

About the Author

D Nasir was born in Dayton, Ohio and began writing poetry in the early 1970's. Since then he has written over 2000 poems, 15 manuscripts, 28 short stories, 2 children books, and 16 plays.

He is also an artist who has developed his own unique style of Decoupage art. He studied fine arts at Sinclair and Wilmington colleges, in Ohio and has works of art on display at Antioch College, and at the Paul Laurence Dunbar Memorial House.

Writers can sometimes be just ordinary people, but to be a great writer you must be dedicated and constantly striving to improve upon the skills of the craft you have chosen. D Nasir is a great writer. With every project he completes he asks himself, "How can I make this better?" And so he constantly improves with each book he writes.

The Dust Bubble is one of many books written by D Nasir, but it is his first to be published and also the first of his "*Bones Series Trilogy*", a three-book series about the life of the character, Bones. The other two books of this series is titled, "*Finesse*", and "*Just Don't Fold*". However the story of Bones begins with "*The Dust Bubble*" which introduces Little Chicken Bones when he is just 13 years of age and coming into manhood, while "Finesse", the second book in the series, finds Bones as a grown man who is deep into the street life that he was introduced to as a teenager, and the third book, "*Just Don't Fold*" unfolds the life that Bones calls his square life where he deals with personal issues of his friends and family.

www.ingramcontent.com/pod-product-compliance
Ingram Content Group UK Ltd.
Pitfield, Milton Keynes, MK11 3LW, UK
UKHW041846190726
13854UKWH00002B/747

9 781425 145118